"Can I get your number?"

"Can you have my baby, baby? Be a millionaire."

Nyka rolled her eyes. If there was one thing that never changed, it was that niggas gonna nigga. She sat in the club, pissed and drunk, with a look that practically screamed LEAVE ME THE FUCK ALONE!

But do niggas ever listen? No. One after another after another after another...they all stepped up, and one by one they all got put down like the scrubs they were. What was it about thirsty negroes and clubs anyway, that they always honed in on the most heartbroken bitches? They were nappy headed moths attracted to a flame.

Well, Nyka was one bitch wasn't having that shit tonight. *I might be lonely, but this pussy ain't desperate enough for any ol' musty dick.* She knocked back another swig of Remy and took in her surroundings at the club.

Her club. No matter what some fuckboy nigga wanted to say about it otherwise.

Dante's was poppin fire as usual, full of niggas and broads, players and hoes, all dancing or drinking or flirting or DL fucking. From the second level bar

Chapters

Nyka
Trigga
Nyka
Derryk
TRIGGA
NYKA
TRIGGA
NYKA
TRIGGA
WILD
VEEDA
CRUX
NYKA
TRIGGA
WILD
TRIGGA
NYKA
VEEDA

I can't even deny—I've been
BLESSED. Blessed with the ability

and the opportunity to tell stories for people to enjoy. Praise be to God, my family, and to all my readers, without whom none of this is possible.

Coming Soon From Rae C.

Ride For My Trigga

Bae Better Have My Money

Sign up <u>HERE</u> to receive updates on new releases!

CHAPTER ONE

Nyka

"Can I get you a drink?"

where she sat, she could see it all in red and blue and green and orange, the color of the lights brightly strobing the floor. Nyka let it all set in and closed her eyes, lost in the beats of Drake's *Shot for Me.*

I can see it in your eyes: you're angry

Regret got shit on what you're feeling now

The lyrics penetrated her psyche, vibrated the deepest part of her membrane, and she tried to let them take her away to someplace else. Someplace where a woman like her--a down chick, a loyal broad--someone like her didn't have to feel like the first bitch eliminated on a rerun of *Flavor of Love*. Someplace where she'd be appreciated by the man lucky enough to receive her heart, her body, her soul.

But no matter how hard she tried, her mind kept going back to the muthafucker who did her wrong.

Fuck Derryk. Fuck. That. Nigga. Nyka didn't deserve to have her heart broken, her dreams shattered. Not like this. Not after everything she'd done for him. Dante's might've been his dream, but it was her sweat. She'd helped build the joint up from a mere concept, a fucking seed. She'd helped raise it from a raggedy hole in the wall, then to a sweaty lodge that couldn't afford to serve more than watered Cristal, all the up to *this*. And in a few months, construction would begin on Dante's Inferno, nine rooms of clubbing, gambling, and all around debauchery, located in the heart of the 'Sip. Sitting next to the biggest casino in the mid-South, it was guaranteed money. She knew in her heart that it was going to be the biggest, baddest place south of Memphis.

Fuck Derryk if he thought he'd push her out of this venture for some Gulf Coast trick.

"Sup, baby, you look like you need some..." started another scrub from the left, approaching her all stealth, like a broke-down ninja. Nyka shot him a look of cold malice, turning him on his heels mid-sentence. Forget hooking up, she wanted that nigga flaccid, to not even be able to beat his meat when he got back home.

"You *better* run," she mumbled on behalf of her shitty mood and broken-hearted bitches everywhere.

Fuck niggas!

She looked around for KD, the bartender. Nyka needed a refill of poison, and she needed that shit *now* if she was going to go through what she had planned.

KD was an unreliable thot if there ever was one, someone who'd have been fired on her first day if not for Derryk's intervention ("We need to be raising sistas up!") and the fact that that she was eye candy for male customers. Blind niggas, Nyka reasoned. Filling out booty shorts was the only experience she'd ever have on her resume. Come to think of it, those facts were probably all related. Derryk's resistance to fire her and KD's thottish ways.

Although Nyka never once suspected anything enough to call the nigga out on it. Nyka wasn't threatened by thirsty bitches. Bad bitches don't feel paranoia. But now that Derryk had revealed himself to be a cheating ass fuckboy, everything was open to reexamination. Who knows what had gone on between the two of them behind Nyka's back?

Nyka stopped herself from even going there. She was all up in her own head.

She slammed her glass down hard to get the attention she deserved. KD stood at the other end of the bar, bent over, her shorts practically a thong, her goodies all up in the face of some man. The bartender rolled her neck in Nyka's direction and motioned for the brotha to wait a moment. She then sashayed to Nyka with a shit-eating grin.

"Don't you think you've had enough, Nyk-Nyk?" she said, using a name she damn well knew Nyka didn't like.

"If I wanted to be called by a little girl's name I'd take my ass back to preschool. Besides, I think this grown woman knows her limits better than you do, *Kentricia*," Nyka shot back using the name KD hated everyone to know. "I thank you to hit me up until I tell you not to."

"Just trying to look out for my girl."

It took all Nyka had not to slap a trick. They weren't girls. They weren't friends. It was a stretch to even call them associates. It was strictly a big boss/dumb employee relationship. "I appreciate that, *buddy*. But as long as I'm signing your checks, best do what I say. 'K?" Nyka said, fake-grinning with all the energy she could muster in the face of bullshit.

"I hear that might not be long..." KD muttered with a smirk, acting as if she knew the secrets of the universe. Nyka stopped mid-sip and glared at her.

"What the hell does that mean?"

"Oh, nothing much," KD responded as she casually wiped the jet-black bar surface of non-existent crumbs. "I just hear you about to cash out, girl. Gonna get paid for your share of this place."

"Oh really? And where'd you hear that?"

"Big Man himself." KD nodded towards the door at the far corner of the joint, on the second level opposite the bar. "I hear that when we open Dante's Inferno, we gon' have a Gulf Coast flavor."

"You sure hear a whole damn lot, bitch," Nyka said, adding extra emphasis to the word so KD knew exactly where things stood. "Don't believe all that mess."

"Hey, don't be mad at the messenger," KD continued as she started back towards the man on the other end of the bar. "I heard that chatter straight from the horse's mouth. In fact, I think there's a meeting going on right now."

Meeting right now? Nyka turned back to the dimly lit office door and involuntarily felt inside her Chanel purse. *This nigga must got me fucked.*

The reality of the situation put Nyka right back in her feelings, now at a level she'd never been before. She sat broken. Defeated. Weak bitch tripping was something new to her, and it had her reeling.

Nyka Sinclair prided herself on being the definition of strong, black, and female. She didn't break the mold; she remade it in her image.

How many chicks could miss an entire year of high school and still get into college at age 18? How many could work 40 hours a week in a factory and never miss a single homework assignment? How many could support themselves by age 20 without a mama's help, with a father long dead? How many could hold it down all the way through business school without a sugar daddy lifting her up or a dirty dick pulling her down?

Despite that will, when she met Derryk, with his swirling brown eyes, his soft baby skin, those perfectly cut arms, it was an exercise in futility. He was a persistent brother who knew what he wanted, and Nyka was game he had locked in his sights. She wasn't normally the one for the alpha type, but brotha had dreams. Ambitions. A black man in Mississippi with good looks, a solid hustle, and a plan? Nyka never stood a chance.

When they finally hooked up, when Nyka let him lay the pipe for the first time--her first time giving up the goods ever--she knew she was tapped out. She'd been blessed, but not as much as he'd been blessed with *her*. Nyka had given up a little of herself, but her core was still intact. She hadn't let a man take away her strength, she'd let him see it to full effect.

And when she inherited her Nana's land when she died, the land Nana earned for being a loyal side-chick to a rich Indian for most of her life, there was never a question of what needed to be done. They broke ground less than three months later, and Dante's was born. Together she and Derryk built and rebuilt the club, each time bigger and better than before. The final evolution would be Dante's Inferno.

But Derryk had other plans. Oh, Dante's Inferno was happening, all right. But he had no plans for Nyka to be a part of it.

Her head swam as she thought about their last conversation.

"Bae, it's done," he said, his voice cold and dismissive, as if he were just talking to an employee he was about to bounce.

"This doesn't make any sense, Derryk. We're partners. Lovers!"

"Not anymore, Nyka." He tried to look off to her side, avoiding her glare. "I've been seeing this chick for a few weeks now. She's down with my vision and she's going to finance all of it. We buying you out."

Nyka would've held her breath if she were actually capable of breathing. It was over? He was buying her out? "You..you can't do that! This land belongs to me! Half this club belongs to me! You can't push me aside for some..some hoe!"

He finally looked her directly in her eyes. "I can, and I will. You'll be well compensated."

Nyka involuntarily rubbed the engagement ring on her finger, now worthless bling. She stoned her face. She'd be damned if she let him see her cry. "And what if I say no?"

Derryk stepped up to her slowly, until they were body to body. "I already made the deal, Bae. I already okayed it with the Choctaws.

"And these Gulfport cats that my new girl runs with? These are not people you say no to."

Nyka shook herself back to the present. Eyes fixed on Derryk's office door, she took out her phone and dialed his line, waiting for a response. Nothing. She changed tactics and texted him. *Nd 2 tlk. Cum out & tlk 2 me lke a man. Dnt mk me bang on ur door.*

She squeezed her eyes shut and tried to regain a grip of this drama going out of control. Nobody could make her do anything. She wasn't selling shit, and she sure as hell wasn't going anywhere. Nobody controlled her life except her, and she refused to give up what she knew was a good thing. She wasn't the type to waste opportunities or throw away relationship. She lived her life a loyal rider, through and through.

Derryk had just momentarily lost his mind. She'd wait out the storm until he came back to his senses. When she opened her eyes, she caught her reflection in the bar mirror behind the bottles and glasses, old, tired, grayed, and used up. Slamming down her fist, she looked again and the real Nyka was back. *I'm not my momma,* she said to herself.

She glanced to her right to everyone at the bar. They'd all seen her mini-breakdown but pretended they didn't. Knowing KD witnessed her moment of weakness pissed her off the most, though.

But Nyka wasn't worried. She'd have something for KD's fresh ass when it was all said and done.

While surveying the scene, the brotha KD had spent most of the night eye-fucking came into focus. Even in the dimness, his fineness wasn't in question. Dark cocoa skin with defined features that included cheekbones you could cut a bitch with, he had exotic features you'd identify with an island nigga. Nyka had messed with a Caribbean guy a few times in college, and she'd almost fallen for his casual cool.

Nyka was so caught up in her tipsy thoughts that she forgot not to stare. The brotha stared back, and broke the stillness between them with a confident grin. Perfect white teeth showed between his dark lips, lips from even 20 feet away Nyka could tell was good at whatever jobs they decided to do.

As bad as he was from afar, Nyka figured he must've been something fierce up close, considering KD had gone out of her way to not only be his new best friend, but to go and fetch him a cup of coffee *in a muthafucking bar.*

Like her Nanny used to say: the thirst be real, babygirl.

The things some hoes did for dick. The man began to sip his brew, and Nyka forced herself to look away.

Spite had never been one of Nyka's traits. Had she been a more unscrupulous broad, she'd be all over this guy in her man's bar. A fine man like that, she'd lead over to Derryk's office door and let fuck her against it.

But that wasn't her in her DNA. Loyalty until death. She'd never let herself become another Sister Treece. She'd never become her mother.

As the DJ changed the tune to Chris Brown's *Dat Night*, Nyka took a few deep breaths and regained herself. Even though she could feel the glare of the dark stranger still boring though her, chipping at her will, her loyalty to Derryk remained strong. Even if Derryk didn't want her, she was still his. She'd given all of her heart to him, and if he took that away there was nothing left. There'd be hell to pay.

Her Nana had always warned her that bitches in their family were crazy, now Nyka knew for sure. As she felt around for the cold steel of her Daddy's old revolver in her purse, she vowed Derryk would pay for breaking her heart by getting a bullet ripped through his.

CHAPTER TWO

Trigga

Trigger was all about the job. Nothing more, nothing less.

His was not to question the reasons. He didn't care about motives or circumstances. He wasn't the one for having a sympathetic ear, and mercy sure as hell wasn't his friend.

He was all about doing the work tasked to him, whether that work came from high or from low, from his cousin or from even God himself. It kept things pure. Kept his perspective untainted.

Make no mistake about it, Trigga stayed one of a kind in that respect. Maybe other cats in his line of work tried to be the same way, to fake that level of objectivity and professionalism, but they always fell short for one reason or another. You couldn't be a hitter when your heart cared only about the money, or the women, or the fleeting thrill. Leave that for the low level street boys.

What mattered to Trigga was destiny. He'd get his assignment, go to Mama Juju, have her read the signs, and if everything fell into place, he'd take the job. No more questions asked. No more answers needed. He'd do so because something bigger than himself demanded it. Trigga didn't think of himself as some hoodrat killer; he was the hand of Fate.

Find. Murk. Move on. Let homies at the Pearly Gates so1 out at the end.

It was fate and the job that had led him to Dante's that night. Sweet place. He'd been to bigger joints, better joints, but he had to admit the atmosphere here was on point. He could immediately see why Crux wanted to move in. Cuz knew a good opportunity when he smelled it. In the middle of still back-asswards Mississippi, Dante's was the type of melting pot America had seemed to the Haitian OGs he grew up around, the ones his Papa and uncles used run their grind with. Black, white, Indian...they were all packed into

Dante's, bumping bodies and trading sweat, all lost in the hard bass pounding through the floor and walls.

Everybody was getting theirs. Everybody was having a good time.

This was the type of place that could make people very, very rich.

He'd made his way up to the second level bar, close enough to the owner's box and where he could have a bird's eye of everything going on below. Trigga liked to be aware of his surroundings, of all the entrances and exits, of the security and anyone else who might

get in his way. He was a man
enjoyed ultimate control.

While sipping and scoping, it
wasn't long before the bartender--
a nicely stacked, cinnamon
flavored dish--had sought him out.

"What'll be your weakness
tonight, Daddy?" ol' girl purred
to him, making sure to lean all in
a brotha's grill.

"Actually, baby, what I want
might be a little strange," he
said, making sure to give her his
best Denzel smile.

"Strange? Mmmm. Special
requests are my spe-ci-a-li-ty,"
she said, enunciating each
syllable as she made sure to brush

her fingertips against his
Burberry shirt. "And call me KD."

She was trying too hard, but
that was alright. "Ok, KD," Trigga
responded, letting the space
between them shrink. "How about
you hook a brother up with some
hot tea."

KD cocked her eyebrow with
surprise. "Tea? You for real,
nigga?"

"Or some coffee if you can
find it. I'd be very grateful."
Trigga pulled out a benjamin and
slipped it between her fat
breasts, his eyes still locked
into hers. "I'm a man of...unusual
tastes."

"And I'm a woman of exquisi.
flavor," KD gave up with a wink,
using words Trigga could tell she
wasn't accustomed to. "I think I
can hook you up with some black."

As she got ready to leave him,
Trigga gently grabbed her wrist
and rubbed it. "Oh, and can you do
one thing for me? Bring me the
grinds too.

"Where I'm from, they're a
delicacy."

Giving him a 'you're lucky
you're so damn fine' smirk, KD
nodded. She looked around to make
sure the rest of the bar patrons
were belly up on liquor before
heading to a backroom to fulfill

Trigga's request. Trigga watched as she put a little extra bounce in that derriere, not at all mad at her game, even if he wasn't the least bit interested.

He shook his head and chuckled. True, Trigga didn't do what he did for the women, but at times they were a nice bonus. Blessed with smooth brown skin and strong Haitian features, women flocked to him with little effort. After his first kiss of a girl in the second grade, and the girl's subsequent obsession that bordered on grade school stalking, his mother swore up and down he must be possessed by Erzulie, the spirit of love. How else could you explain an 8 year old stealing her Daddy's Rolex to give a boy whose wrist was no bigger than a beanstalk?

Sure, there had always been bigger brothers and richer ones, but when it came to pulling, and pulling well, nobody could touch Trigga St. Croix. And being able to get women to do what he wanted came in handy in his line of work.

This KD chick? He hadn't even worked up a sweat. Having her get him a cup of coffee on a busy night at a bar? Even Trigga had to smile at that. There was good, and there was *good*.

Still, unusual requests weren't something he wanted to make a habit of. Anything to bring attention to himself was bad. That was common sense. No one can snitch up somebody they never notice.

But *she* had made him have to change it up. The she being the bird who sat at the other end of the bar downing shots like a thirsty fish on a hot beach. Trigga had only got a partial look at her at first, but now that his attention wasn't being hogged by Ms. Needy-as-hell-bartender, he saw her for all her glory. She was like a living checklist for what he desired in a lady: soft complexion, juicy lips, long hair, and bumps for days. The lace mini-dress ensemble she wore spoke to her class, despite her drinking like a hoodrat that particular night.

He'd seen this woman before. He'd seen her in his dreams. He'd seen himself making love to her, melting her beneath the white hot glare of his stare, turning her on and then turning her out. She'd been the woman surrounded by a litter of his seed.

Maybe it had only been a dream, but ever since what went down with his Papa those many years ago, Trigga always listened to his dreams.

While Trigga believed in fate, he had never relied on it concerning affairs of the heart. But there was something about *this chick right here* that made him want to believe. Hmmm. It drove him crazy, filled him with an anxiousness he wasn't used to. Had he told his mama how he felt, she'd tell him he was at the crossroads. *Watch out, Trigga, this little girl is about to change your life.*

So he made his mind and sent KD off to get what he needed to figure out what to do next.

"Here you go, Big Daddy," KD said as she brought him a cup of hot water and a side of coffee grinds. "Maybe you'd like some cream to go with that. I can get you some from the back if you want to come for...with me," the chick said while bending all the way forward, breast practically spilling on in his drink. Her desperation was suddenly a major turnoff now that Trigga had spotted the woman of his destiny.

"Maybe later, love. Looks like someone else needs you first," he said, pointing to his dream woman who was clearly trying to get KD's attention.

"Just a moment," she sighed, leaving Trigga with his steaming water and coffee grinds. He used the opportunity to quickly mix the two. Saying a silent prayer, he stirred, stopped, and let a few seconds pass for the grinds to finally settle. Then he poured the dark liquid into an empty shot glass, leaving only the grinds below.

A dark skinned man sitting on the stool next to Trigga, tipsy but still curious, looked on with interest. Since the last thing Trigga needed was to make a scene, he let it go but had his muscles on standby in case he had to slyly knock a busybody out.

"Something wrong with your neck that you can turn it in the direction of your own muthafuckin business?" a voice from the other

side directed at the nosy dude.
Brah got the message and begin to
mind his own.

Trigga turned to his partner,
irritated. "What the hell are you
doing up here, Wild?"

"Just checkin up, homey. You
haven't given a nigga any kind of
signal."

"You know what that means,
right? To sit tight and wait like
you're supposed to do."

"Man, please. You sittin' up
here fuckin around with that
voodoo shit and you want to geek
on me? You better squash that
shit," Wild said, leaning back

against the bar, looking on at the scene below.

Trigga never worked with partners, and he hated hard-headed young bucks looking to come up. He'd had no choice but to bring Wild with him, however, seeing as though he was Crux's nephew and he wanted to know if Wild had the chops. Tall and lanky, with high yellow skin that looked perpetually rashed up, Wild looked every bit his street name, and acted even worse.

Trigga grabbed him by the arm, and he felt Wild tense up. Stupid kid was always ready to jump on someone, whether it be a friend or foe. "Listen up, Wild. I'm runnin' this. I got the entire level scoped. You do your job and d up the lower level. If you can't follow orders, me and Crux are going to have words about your future in the chain of command."

Wild jerked his arm away, the message clear. He gave the now returned KD a wink and an air kiss before he headed back below.

"Friend of yours?" she asked Trigga.

"Just somebody from back in the scene." Yet another thing to sorry about: KD connecting his face with Wild's. He was about to make a mental note to deal with her too, when he finally read the grinds at the bottom of his cup.

The infinite lover. He squinted his eyes and looked again, ignoring KD's tapping of his shoulder. The sign was still there. Trigga looked over and saw his future wife momentarily looking at him. His heart quickened and he gave her an awkward smile, his game momentarily off. She turned away.

The wolf in Trigga got ready to pounce.

"I said, what's your name Daddy?" KD interrupted his thoughts yet again, this time her

tired ass much too close to his
ear for comfort.

"Noneya."

"Ohhh. What is that, African?"

Trigga gave her an 'Are you
serious?' look and poured the
coffee back into its original mug
and got up.

"I think I'll go over there
and handle some business. Why
don't you reup my friend right
here?" Trigga said to the confused
KD as he nodded to the fella who'd
just been up in his business.

Fate was a helluva broad,
Trigga thought to himself as he

started to walk to the fine black
queen he was about to make his.

CHAPTER THREE

Nyka

Nyka stewed in her thoughts about her broken heart, and the craziness it could do to a bitch, when she felt a new presence next to hers.

"There's no shame in admitting you've had too much," the fine ass negro from across the bar said as he sat on the stool next to her's. His voice was smooth bass, sending a shiver through her body. From afar, he had been fine; up close, brother was magnifique. His dark, cut features were on full display in Dante's dim light. Clothes that had to have been tailored by foreign sounding niggas clung to his body. If that wasn't enough, he smelled like the type of man

you could imagine fucking a sister
until her insides swelled. A
stallion muthafucker.

Of course he was cocky as
fuck.

"This is the second time some
muthafucker had tried to tell me
what I can or cannot put in my
mouth. Maybe you should worry
about me sticking my shoe up in
yours for not minding your own,"
she said through a haze of
tipsiness and intrigue.

"Whoa, whoa, whoa," he said,
laying his cup down and raising
his hands in mock surrender. "No
need to swear at your man, little

Ma. Those lips are way too pretty for such a dirty mouth."

Nyka smiled inwardly at his slick comeback, even though she was getting annoyed at his audacity. "There you go again telling me what I can do with my mouth. And since when the fuck did you become my man?"

"I guess you're right that I'm not your man. Otherwise you wouldn't have such a problem with me telling you what to do with that mouth," he said, grinning. Nyka rolled her eyes and craned her neck so he couldn't see her grin. This slick fool was something else.

"How about this, little Ma? Why don't we be friends? My name is Trigga." He reached out his hand to shake her.

Reluctantly, Nyka shook it. "I'm Nyka."

Trigga flashed what she could've sworn was a surprised, nervous look before settling back into his confident facade.

"Your parents gave you a beautiful name, Nyka."

"Whatever. Just because you know my name doesn't mean you'll get a chance to know any of the body parts that answer to it. Understood?"

"Understood, little Ma. I'm just tryna get to know somebody new."

Trigga had game, Nyka had to admit. She awkwardly played with the glass of Remy in her hand, aware that he'd yet to take his eyes off of her. "Can you not stare at me?"

"Kinda hard not to, but okay."

Broken hearts breed desperate chicks, Nyka reminded herself. While this Trigga cat was indeed interesting, she was and always would be a loyal chick. One love, one man, one life had been her motto ever since her mama had destroyed her Daddy and broken her home. It didn't matter how suddenly warm Trigga made her pussy feel as he casually brushed her arm, as far as she was concerned her kitty was stamped with a capital D for Derryk.

"Little Ma, I hope you don't mind, but I make it a habit to read people. It goes with my line of work. And I'm sensing you're a woman in a lot of pain," he said with what she could tell was care.

Was she so obvious? Nyka opened and closed, opened and closed her mouth, unsure of what to say next. No doubt she was in pain, and she wanted and needed to let it out.

Nobody knew what had gone down between her and Derryk. For one thing, she was too embarrassed to tell anyone, even her girl Red. And for another, Nyka always kept her troubles to herself. It was a product of being in a broken home, of being judged because of the ratchedness of her mother. She'd learned to protect herself by not giving the finger-pointers any more ammo to use against her.

In truth, Nyka couldn't completely close off, but she *did* come across as standoffish. That invisible wall of psyche had protected her for a lot of years, until she had finally let Derryk in. Now that he'd breached it and

trashed the place, that same wall
threatened to collapse upon her,
to make her have to claw her way
out.

She felt alone. There was no
one left she could reach for.

Until this smooth talking,
drawers-wetting playa.

"I don't think you want my
troubles."

"Try me."

And so she told him her
troubles. Not everything, but the
gist. And when she was too tired
to talk for a minute, he let her
sip on his strong, black,
bittersweet cup of brew. It didn't

escape her notice that the coffee was a lot like him, smooth and warm, giving her the strength needed to come back from the brink of where she had been just a little while earlier. When she could finally continue, he caressed her wrists, listening and not judging, until she was finally finished with her sorry tale.

"I'm a sad ass bitch, aren't I?"

"Not at all, lil Ma. You the type to give all of your heart, even if that means it can be stole or broken. Any real man would be down with that."

Hearing someone other than herself recognize that fact felt like someone lifting her from the grave. Before she knew it, she was nudging her leg close to his. He used the opportunity to caress her soft legs, messaging thighs that had been strained from trying to lift an entire world.

"If you ask me, a smart bitch would've known her man didn't want her and seen herself for the side bitch she is," KD broke in. Bitch was sour as all fuck having hovered around Nyka and Trigga the whole time while pretending to tidy up. Ever since Trigga's dismissal, KD fumed and let Nyka know as much through her actions.

Every few seconds she'd sent evil glances Nyka's way. Had Nyka not been so into her conversation with Trigga, she'd put that mess on lock immediately.

"It seems that you got the same problem, little bird. But I don't think anyone would claim you to be smart enough to know that anyway," Trigga shot back, before Nyka had the chance to lay fists on that ass.

"Now go do you job and live long enough to enjoy that c-note I threw your way," Trigga finished in a tone not even KD's dumb ass dared to ignore. She walked away mumbling, what little sense she had enough to warn her from crossing the nigga she'd previously been ready to fuck.

"Sorry you had to see that, lil Ma. I hate when people run their trap too much, and I'd have hated you to mess up your classy disposition dealing with it."

Nyka chuckled at his cheesy ass before forcing herself to get real. She was attracted to Trigga, no doubt about that. But nothing could come of it, right? There was unfinished business with Derryk that took priority.

"So what are you going to do about your man?" Trigga said, seemingly reading her mind.

Nyka looked at Trigga and a bit of sadness set in. Her time with him had been better than any with Derryk for what felt like years. But she'd made a promise to herself.

"Derryk and I have unfinished business."

"What kind of business?"

Nyka unconsciously reached for her purse as if it were a security blanket. She hoped Trigga didn't notice. Her Daddy's revolver still sat inside, waiting for the moment to present itself if her meeting with Derryk didn't go the way she had hoped.

"I need closure, and if possible, I want to try to make it work with him. Derryk and I have been together for a long time, and I can't just let those emotions go that easy."

Trigga stroked her cheek with her thumb. "I wouldn't expect anything less from someone special like you. But do me a favor and give me your phone."

She took her phone from her purse and handed it to him.

"Imma give you my digits, lil Ma. When this all breaks out, one way or another, you give me a call just to let me know you alright. Gotta look out for my new friend."

"Okay...friend," Nyka said sheepishly, as she reached for her phone. In the process of grabbing it, the phone slipped from her hand, hitting the floor. 'Oh lord, please don't have lost his number' went through her mind as she crouched to pick up the phone. She instantly felt guilty for the thought. It didn't do anything for her guilt seeing the outline of dick through his pants on the way back up.

"You okay, lil Ma," Trigga cheesed her.

"Yeah, just lost my balance for a second."

"Uh-huh."

She looked back at Derryk's office door one more time, feeling better about herself now that she'd met such a fine nigga who thought she was worth more than she thought of herself. She gathered her courage.

"I'm going to go over there and knock on that door and get this shit over with." Saying it was half the battle, she figured, and she felt her knees wobble as she got up. She took a few steps, feeling weaker with each one. Her greatest fear was that by the time she reached Derryk, she'd be that broken broad she'd been just a few hours earlier.

She felt the pull of Trigga's hand on her arm.

"How bout you wait here with me. Your man has to come out of his hole eventually. Until then you can sit here with me having your back."

Nyka nodded at the perfect sounding plan, caught up in her feelings for a brotha she suddenly wanted but knew she could never have, and a nigga she was bound to, good or bad, but who no longer wanted her.

In the end, she was going to be all alone. Life was a fucking trip.

CHAPTER FOUR

Derryk

"Goddammit, D! Eat that pussy!"

She didn't need to say it twice. Derryk was already all in. The normally cool and composed Veeda lost control, and Derryk loved every second of it. He pushed up on her legs, lifting those sexy thighs even higher on his shoulders, and got a better view of her kitty. So wet. Veeda kept that shit shaved, just the way he liked it. Nyka? Derryk had to beg that broad to shave hers, and even then it was never as pretty as the tinder box gushing in his face right now.

Licking his lips, Derryk dove back in, getting juicy fruit all

over his grill. He started slowly
from the bottom of her slit,
moving his tongue up and down
methodically. Veeda's pussy
contracted with each motion,
squeezing a little gush out each
time, until there was enough to
not only drip down her ass crack
but cover his neatly trimmed
beard.

"Uhnnnnn!" she moaned, that
shit already too good for words.

After a while, Derryk moved up
to that clit. He felt Veeda
stiffen as the broad side of his
tongue began to concentrate on the
hard nub. He went back and forth,
back and forth, the sweetness of
Veeda's juices making the perfect

lubricant. After he she finally relaxed, he went for the shocka and started sucking on her knob.

He knew he hit the spot when she started to convulse under his mouths grip. Now that he had her where he wanted, Derryk slid his index finger inside, gorging her pussy until finally settling upon the rough patch of her g-spot. The combination of his suction and his finger was driving a bitch to her to the brink, and Derryk showed no signs of letting up.

Veeda squeezed her thighs around his head like a vise, and began to rock with the movement of his tongue. Derryk didn't mind, though. It only spurred him on. He grabbed her legs and forced them wide, giving his face all the room it needed to bring her to come.

"Aaaahhh!" she spasmed, trying to mute her cries by biting on a pencil that was within her reach. Derryk stood up and looked at his handiwork.

Veeda was a bad ass bitch, with chocolate brown skin, big titties, and a big, soft ass to bring it all together. She lay on his desk, disheveled but still classy as all fuck, her chest going up and down as she tried to catch her breath.

The way she wore her Jason Wu dress gave Derryk had a hard time controlling his dick. He'd always dreamed about fucking high class, and he couldn't imagine any higher class than Veeda. She had it all: the looks, the smarts, a phat ass, and most of all, a hefty bank roll. He was already smitten with a bitch, and he'd only been hitting it for a few weeks.

Naw, she didn't love a nigga back. Not yet. But she would when she saw the money they were about to make. He'd already made room on his throne for her, dumping Nyka like the bad habit she'd become. When Veeda had proposed to buy into Dante's and helped take the idea for Dante's Inferno to the next level, he knew he'd met his soul mate. Once they were making paper together, they'd be ready to make babies together.

After a good second, Veeda got up and put on her panties. As she bent, Derryk couldn't help but thank god for putting something so sexy on this earth. He could tell that she knew he was enjoying the view, as she slowly made a show of it. Derryk had never been a leg man, but the way her strappy platform sandals made her calves pop sent a shiver down his spine.

"You sure do have a talented tongue, Mr. Jones," she said, checking her make up in the corner mirror.

"Momma always said my slick mouth would get me into places," he said, licking the pussy juice on his fingers.

He rushed her to give her a kiss on the neck, but she craned back, placing her index finger over his lips. "Now that we have pleasure out of the way, we need to discuss business."

Derryk backed away and let Veeda comb her long hair, as long and as straight as any Indian's. That it was real was the shit as far as Derryk was concerned. He knew it wasn't the time to gawk, though. It was time to put his game face on, and let her know how real her man could truly be.

"Like I was telling you before, I got shit on check around here. I let Nyka know how it was going to be."

"And how did she take it?"

"The fuck you think she took it? Ultimately it don't matter. Nyka has and always will do whatever I ask her to, no matter if she doesn't want to."

"You sound mighty confident there," Veeda said as she slowly walked to him, her face slightly lowered seductively. Taking the tip of her finger, she stroked his cheek. "Maybe that slick mouth ain't as good as you think it is."

She walked away and sat on his office couch.

"The fuck that supposed to mean?" Derryk asked, feeling like his game was being challenged.

Veeda cocked her head as if sizing him. "Doesn't mean anything more than what I said. You just told this woman of yours that you don't love her anymore, that you want her to sign away her inheritance to this land and her stake in this club. Are you that damn sure you got her under your control?"

"Let me tell you something," Derryk started, feeling the need to break it down. "Nyka's been eating outta my hand since the day we met. I had her giving up the pussy on our first date when she was still god-fearing virgin. I was whispering in her ear about building this club the day after her grandmother died and left it to her. I got this under control."

Veeda twisted her mouth into a crooked grin and raised her hand in surrender. *The fuck this broad coming at me with all this shit?* Derryk thought to himself.

He knew the deal. He understood the risks. Veeda's people were not to be trifled with. He'd never met or talked to the cats, but he'd heard enough rumors from his people around.

Gulf Coast gangstas were hard core, and when they wanted in on some action, they either made it happen or they burned everything to the ground.

"So when are we going to make Dante's Inferno happen, baby girl?"

Veeda put her glasses back on, making her look the consummate professional. "As soon as you come up with the paperwork. I'm assuming you've let your ex know she needs to bring that post haste."

Even though the fancy talk was a turn on, Derryk was beginning to get a bit pissed at Veeda doubting his ability. She damn well knew he'd let Nyka know to bring the papers ASAP. What kind of dumb as fuck boy did she think he was?

Derryk wasn't no dumb ass negro who didn't know how to hustle. He'd thought up of Dante's in a dream of some old ass literature he'd read when he was in high school. The first version of the club had been some four wall piece of shit straight out a horror flick, but within weeks it became a prime jump off for miles around.

It was no accident, neither. Derryk was a natural businessman, a to-the-bone hustler just like his daddy and his granddaddy before him. Not even a year after the first Dante's opened its doors, he'd built another, and then another, and finally this current version which would've made most people in his position fat and happy.

Not Derryk though. His ultimate dream was something bigger: Dante's Inferno.

And after working his fingers to the bone for so many years, that dream was within reach. Dante's Inferno would be situated in prime territory next to the Choctaw reservation and the nearby Indian casinos. It was going to be an all-in-one entertainment hot spot, built in the side a sloping ridge of land inherited by Nyka from her uppity ass grandmother he was glad finally died. Dante's Inferno would be nine levels, with six above ground and three below. Each descending level would cater to a new vice. It would have sports betting, s smoker's lounge, bar, dance club, a mini-casino, private gaming, a gentleman's club, VIP, and the 'anything goes' Ninth Level. To top it off, the broad side of the joint would overlook one of the sweetest looking creeks to be found in the whole damn Deep South.

It was going to be *tight*. He had it all planned: the design, the lighting, the material, even the color of the water in the toilets. Knowing you can't be any kind of real playa in the rackets game without the blessing of the local squaws, he even had Choctaw investors and a 'in principle' agreement with the Choctaw nation. They'd provide the machines, and he'd make sure those green dollars kept flowing into the proper red hand.

All a nigga needed was the paperwork to make it official.

"Baby, we'll get this handled *tonight*," he said to reassure himself as well as Veeda. He grabbed his phone and saw he had messages.

Evidently Nyka was there tonight. Good. Maybe God really was looking out for him.

One way or another tonight was the night Nyka met her fate.

CHAPTER FIVE

TRIGGA

"I see you met a new friend."

Nyka damn near dropped her glass when she heard the voice. Trigga looked up at the source, a light shaded clown who did his best to hide the anger beneath his skin. Although he'd never met the dude, Trigga immediately knew who it was.

Derryk Jones.

Trigga had memorized that stupid mug, and it amused him to see him so put off by Trigga's presence. *Right feelings, wrong reason*, Trigga thought to himself. He leaned back against the bar, relaxed and without feelings, and politely nodded. Trigga gave an easy smile to let the man know he was less than a concern to him at that moment.

The same couldn't be said of Nyka. Trigga noticed how tense she'd suddenly become, her hand instinctively reaching for her purse. Girl was ready to pop off. Trigga placed his hand on her back in support, hoping to level her out before she tried to do something stupid.

"I see you got a new one too," Nyka finally responded, standing to get a better look at the woman a few steps behind Derryk.

The woman carried a cocky smile as she approached. "Just make sure this gets done tonight," she said to Derryk, passing through on her way to the exit, winking at Nyka and Trigga in the process. Although she and Trigga met eyes, he kept he carefree demeanor. He didn't want anyone knowing he was suddenly as tense as Nyka had been just a few seconds prior.

The hell was Veeda doing there? he wondered. *Crux hadn't mentioned it.* Nothing about the job was running right. Trigga didn't like surprises, and at some point he'd figure out Veeda's role in any of this, but for right now it was Nyka and Derryk that demanded his attention.

The two stared at each other, neither one giving an inch. Trigga silently wished he'd have been able to get Nyka out of the club before this confrontation. The conversation between them had been so tight that he'd lost track of time and the job.

Nyka was an adamant broad, seemingly hell bent to stay loyal to a clown who clearly couldn't appreciate the loyalty. It had taken a lot of effort, but he thought he was close to getting her to lay her head down at his place for the night. Now this dude had to show up and ruin it.

"And who the fuck is the nigga, anyway?" Derryk shot at

her, waving his hands in Trigga's direction.

"A *gentleman* who seems to appreciate my company more than my own damn man, evidently. We were just having friendly conversation." Her need to explain herself irritated Trigga.

"You got some nerve pulling that creeping shit up in here, Nyk. I should fucking clown you right now for this."

Nyka let out a high pitched laugh. "Derryk, you must've lost yourself. You're not my man anymore, remember?"

"But this is still my club, and you doing shit like this

embarrasses me. My rep is everything around here!"

"Oh, fuck you. Maybe you should've checked your caked out face before worrying about embarrassment. Get out of here with your bullshit, breath smelling like burnt pussy," she said, sticking her finger to his forehead and pushing. "I'll talk to whoever I please wherever I please. If you don't want me, I can easily find someone who will."

"Whatever bitch," Derryk said, trying to play it off, but Trigga could sense he was this close to doing something stupid. "All I care about is you bringing those papers here so we can get this legal shit straight and clear. This club, this land, belongs to me."

"No, Derryk, this *land* belongs to me, and so does half this club. And I don't think I want to sign shit over to you," she said, her finger back in his chest.

"You better think twice about that." Derryk grabbed her wrist, the veins in his hand pulsing from the effort. With her other hand, Nyka rifled through her purse, the anger on her face replaced by surprise when she found her gun missing. In that split second a wild-eyed Trigga placed his own hand around Derryk's wrist, ready to break it.

"Brother, you gonna have a hard time signing papers when you're missing a hand. No kindly let the lady go."

Trigga suddenly felt all eyes on them. Even the music seemed to stop. Too many people had noticed him already that night, but at that moment he didn't care. Wasn't any man about to lay his hands on any woman around Trigga, and especially not his lil Ma-in-waiting. Visions of a night a long time ago with his Papa flashed in his mind.

Derryk let go, and so did Trigga. A couple of beefy guys in all black wearing 'Security' t-shirts made their way up to the

confrontation, ready to pounce on
Trigga at Derryk's command.

"Get this fool out of here!"
he commanded them, causing Trigga
to square up.

"No! Until something changes,
you two work for me too," Nyka
said, waving them off. She turned
to Trigga. "We were just leaving
anyway."

Trigga smiled at what he knew
was his, and took her by the arm.

"Just be sure to sign my
papers, Nyk. We wouldn't want this
to get ugly, would we?"

It was a clear threat, and one
that Trigga knew he'd have an

answer for. And soon. As they neared the exit, he made sure to lower his hand to Nyka's backside, eliciting looks of hatred from both Derryk and KD.

Climbing down the stairs to the first floor entrance, his eyes met Wild's. The rowdy buck gave him a cold glare. Trigga hoped he wouldn't do anything stupid in the meantime, until Trigga figured out a way to get their plan involving Derryk back on track.

Once outside in the cold night air, Nyka turned on him sharply, holding out her hand. Trigga smirked and reached behind his back for her revolver. It was impressive that she'd figured out he lifted it off of her when she dropped her phone.

"Sorry I had to do that, but I could tell you were planning to make a terrible mistake. I've seen that look before."

Nyka paused and looked at him curiously. Trigga expected her to be mad as all hell, but there was none of that on her face. Instead she just nodded.

"So what you going to do, Ms. Nyka? You comin' with me?" he asked, hopeful.

She looked down and slowly shook her head. "I need to do some thinking first. But thank you," she said, looking at Trigga with those big doe eyes.

"Aye. You got my number, Ms. Nyka."

As she walked to her car, Trigga checked his new message.

Wild: U need to gve me rundown NOW 4 real. U off ur gme

Dumb young buck. There was nothing to worry about. One way or another, tonight business would be taken care of.

* * *

By the time Trigga got back to his hotel suite, it was already past midnight. He checked his phone again, but there was no message from Nyka. It was okay. What lil' Ms. Nyka didn't know was fate was on his side. That meant time was too, and a person in Trigga's line of work had to have all the patience in the world.

He unbuttoned his shirt and tuned the sound system to something that could help him unwind.

The smooth rhythms of DeAngelo relaxed him. He never wanted to perform a job while hyped; that was a recipe for mistakes. There was already too many things that

had or could possibly go wrong--
Nyka, Wild, Veeda, the flashbacks
he had at the club--for him to not
do the best he could to be in the
right frame of mind.

Trigga heated up a cup of tea
and sat at the suite's desk. It
was always a trip when people saw
him sipping the stuff like an old
English broad, but he could care
less. The one pleasant memory of
his Papa was that he enjoyed the
stuff too. *Good for the belly,
boy. Good for the brain*, his
father would say in his Haitian
accent.

His old man had been on his
mind too much lately. It was a bad
omen, a sign by the Fates to let

him know he was acting too much like him. Maybe now that he'd found Nyka, that wouldn't happen. Settling down, making roots, a house full of seeds--suddenly that seemed realistic.

He took off his shoes and lay down on the bed. He checked his watch again. He had time before the job needed to be done. Thankfully, he'd received no more messages from Wild. Buck was probably getting some brain from some chick at the club, anyway. Unprofessional. Undisciplined.

Trigga didn't even notice when he fell asleep. Suddenly he was back in Shreveport, a nine year old boy, asleep on his run down bed. Papa was big, imposing, a true Haitian hustler, with hard features and a harder hand. The whippings of his mama had been nothing new, but never this severe.

You been steppin' out on me, bitch?

Horace no! They lying. You know I love you!

He didn't believe. The way Papa was raised, you always put the word of your crew over any woman, and his crew had convinced him his wife was a no good trick.

With no hesitation, he pulled his nine and squeezed on the trigger.

Nine years old, Trigga woke up in sweat. The gift of premonition was something his mama always told him he had, but he'd never believed it until that moment. The sounds of is Papa beating his Mama were clear. It was happening, just like in his dream.

Little Trigga walked to their room, the weight of his fear so heavy it seemed to be pulling him down to hell. His dream played out. Again and again Papa's hand met his mama's face. He saw her face, bloodied and swollen. She looked at him.

As the blood flowed down her face, his mama's face disappeared, replaced by Nyka's.

Papa pulled out his piece, ready to squeeze the trigger...

Trigga woke up with a scream.

He looked at the clock. Dumb. He'd caught himself slipping again.

There was another scream, this time not his, but coming from the suite next door. He knew whose suite it was; there was a reason why he'd requested this exact room.

He heard a man's voice. *You think you can fuck with me, Nyka? I warned you this shit was gonna turn wild on your ass.*

Trigga knew what was about to happen. He strapped himself and ran out the door.

CHAPTER SIX

NYKA

Nyka looked at her watch. A
couple of hours had passed since

she left the club, and her heart still felt as torn as ever. Instead of going home, she'd been sitting in her car, listening to some Erykah Badu, and debating whether to smoke the joint she'd copped off her girl Red to deal with her stress.

It was crazy how much in her feelings a bitch could be. After her encounter with Derryk, Nyka should've been fuming. She should've been ready to take the revolver right back into Dante's and make the whole joint rain hot fire. Take her land? Take her club? Take her dignity and stomp it into the floor? Was he serious? No nigga should've been allowed to do that, especially not to a loyal woman like Nyka. She should've been ready to go to war and leave no bodies unburned.

Yet she'd seen Derryk's face when he'd seen her with Trigga. He was hurt, and most importantly, clearly jealous. It wasn't the reaction of someone who was ready to throw away a good thing, an important portion of his life for some side chick and her check. Giving up on Derryk was something Nyka knew a smart woman would do, but Nyka was feeling anything but smart at that moment.

Then there was the part about him laying hands on her. Her wrist still felt sore, and she rubbed it. No doubt it was an inexcusable act, but in her heart she wanted to believe it was just desperation. He'd made a deal with a Gulf Coast devil, and the nigga had acted out of fear of the consequences. Derryk wasn't thinking straight.

"Fuck that shit."

Nyka smacked her head for even entertaining those excuses. Perspective and perception were a muthafucker when you tried to convince yourself to believe what you wanted to be true. Forgiving some actions like Derryk's, trying to win back a man who didn't want you...that's was some weak-bitch shit, and she'd have said so to the face of any other woman in a similar predicament. It was funny how that shit went down: one woman's weakness was another's virtue, a til-you-die loyalty.

Her momma had messed her up in the head from an early age; she knew that for sure now. Leaving a nigga at his weakest, kicking him when he was down, taking the money and running...that was Sister Treece to a tee. Nyka would die before she would exhibit those traits.

One life, one man. Her motto since those hard days growing up. Why'd Trigga have to show up and make life so difficult? She'd only known the man for a few hours but there was already a connection as deep as any she'd felt with Derryk. It wasn't even just a physical thing--although Trigga's sharp features and soft lips could give any sister palpitations--it was the way he seemed to just *get it*.

He looked at her in ways that, she had to admit, no man had looked at her. Not Derryk, not *anyone*. When shit was about to go down in the club, he was at her back, no questions asked, his strong hand at her back for support. She'd always felt safer around dark-skinned brothers, probably because her Daddy and brother were a couple, and Trigga made her feel like she was wrapped in Kevlar, ready for the bullets to fly.

In the few short moments she'd known him, he'd shown her the loyalty she never thought possible from a man, the same type of ride-or-die enthusiasm that burdened her right now, keeping her from completely giving up on Derryk's dumb ass.

Everything was all twisted. Nyka fired up her blunt and let the smoke fill her lungs. As it sat there, her emotions morphed into a physical thing that flowed down and around her body. She felt light, like taking flight. Exhaling and taking another drag, she stayed up in her thoughts, floating towards Trigga's imaginary arms, not sure if she was ready to melt into them.

Her pussy tingled from the thought of letting go and being handled, of allowing Trigga take her by force. A man like that would have his way with her. He'd dismiss her wishy-washy shit, not take no for an answer. Face down, ass up. *Get ready for the real deal, lil Ma.*

And the fucking? That dick print she'd caught a glance of was no joke; he run her completely out. Maybe that's what she needed. It's sure as hell what she wanted.

A buzzing interrupted her dream.

God damn. She pulled out her phone and read the message. The text was from Derryk, marked urgent. Suddenly he wanted to talk, at his place. He needed to see her *now*.

Nyka sighed and bucked her head against the seat. This shit was unreal in so many ways. Unreal at how he could just pull her strings whenever he wanted. Unreal that she so wanted to be loyal that she's already decided to give him a chance to speak his peace.

She scrolled through her phone to find Trigga's number. Sighing, it occurred to her that maybe some things weren't meant to be.

The right man at the wrong time.

Slapping herself a couple of times to sober up, she started her car.

***

After changing her mind a few times, Nyka finally arrived at the casino hotel. It was a tall, flashy place, the lobby scattered with people full of liquor and jangling with coins. Most were the type to be there at hours of the night before getting up the next morning for Sunday school. Nyka shook her head at one old broad being wheeled in with an oxygen tank, still ready to get bout it with the first slot machine she could find.

They were the type of people Nyka left home to get away from, the Sister Treeces and blinged up deacons of Sunday mornings. The fake people of the world always ready to cast judgment at anyone but themselves.

She got into the elevator and pressed 8. Derryk had been shacked up on the eighth and highest floor since dumping Nyka, a special guest of his Choctaw business partners. As long as he delivered his promises as far as paperwork, Derryk lived life as the Golden Boy. Of course, now it all hinged on whether or not Nyka decided to get with the plan and play ball.

Once on the top floor Nyka exited the elevator and started her slow walk to Derryk's suite. The room number he'd give her was 824, but when she reached 823 she instinctively stopped.

Girl, the weed done fucked you up, she said to herself and moved one door down. Before she could even knock, Derryk opened the door, a glass of liquor in his hand, looking relaxed and freshly clean in a cotton robe.

"Nyk, what took you so long? Damn," he started, and Nyka rolled her eyes and walked past. The scent of Clive Christian--Nyka's favorite cologne--emanated from him. She fought the impulse to rub his bare chest.

"I'm here like you asked, Derryk. What you want to talk about?" she with all the strength she could muster, and sat.

"I'm sorry about the drama tonight. Had a nigga messed up, fucking with someone else in my domain."

"Your domain? It ain't your domain yet. If it were, I wouldn't' be here, now would I?"

"You and your smart mouth again, Nyk."

Nyka signed in frustration. "Derryk, I don't want to fight, okay? Let's just talk. We used to be able to do that." She did want to talk. Clear the air. Make this somehow work, as crazy as it all seemed.

"Do I look like I want to talk?" he said, his face stern. He knelt on the couch beside Nyka and bodied her onto her back. "You put a nigga in some frame of mind tonight with that stunt." He kissed her on her lips, piercing her mouth with an adventurous tongue.

The same tongue he'd been eating someone else's pussy with just a few hours before. Nyka pushed against his body, softly at first, and then with force. He looked at her momentarily and came back at her, moving his assault to her neck and then her chest.

Against her will, Nyka moaned at the onslaught. Her eyes closed, trying to imagine her and Derryk when they were at their best, when the passion was at its hottest. When he was her southern king and she his ride or die queen. She closed her eyes, and instead of Derryk's caramel face, a darker face with harder features and soft lips invaded her thoughts.

She pushed him again, this time hard enough to send herself to the floor. As Nyka pulled herself up, Derryk grabbed her arm and pulled her into his chest.

"The fuck, Nyka?" he said, his faced red.

"I didn't come over here just so you can fuck me and go back to your side bitch!" She jerked away. He started to laugh, malice in his eyes.

"Oh please, Nyka! You've been begging for me to come back, and all I was trying to do is give you what you want. I asked you over here so we could get down one more time for old time's sake. But

since you want to lock you pussy
up on me, fine." While he spoke,
he invaded her space, forcing her
back to the wall. "You don't have
to be my new jump on if you don't
want.

"But you damn well better sign
those papers for me."

As he walked away, Nyka could
feel her blood boil. She'd had
enough of the bullshit. Her? A
side chick to this nigga? "Fuck
you, Derryk! I'm not signing
anything, anywhere, anyplace. You
can tell you Gulf Coast friends
they can kiss my ass!"

He stopped and bowed his head.
Nyka stood, uncertain and uneasy,

as he reached into his robe and turned to her, a nine in his hand aimed straight at her head.

She took off, but before she reached the door she felt a sharp pain in her skull. Fallen to the floor, she looked up at the towering Derryk, realizing he'd pistol whipped the shit out of her.

"You think this is a game? Do you have any idea about the people you fucking with? About what they will do to us?" Derryk's eyes were wild and focused, the look of someone ready to throw down in the street. He cocked his hand and slapped her once, then twice.

"Derryk! Please!"

"Fuck this please business!" he said, ramming the nine into Nyka's face. Vision blurred by blood and tears, Nyka couldn't recognize Derryk anymore as a man. He was an animal ready to rip her apart. "You think you can fuck with me, Nyka? I warned you this shit was gonna turn wild on your ass."

Nyka held up her arms in defense as Derryk pulled back for one more blow.

BOOM.

The sound of the suite door being kicked opening shocked them both. Derryk looked up, his mouth open in surprise, and then in a burst of red his head exploded.

Nyka screamed and scrambled backwards from his heavy body. She slowly turned to look at the doorway, where Trigga stood, his gun still in his hand.

CHAPTER SEVEN

TRIGGA

It had always been Trigga's plan to kill Derryk Jones. Those were his orders, and fate decreed it to be in the right. He hadn't expected to meet Nyka along the way, and damn straight didn't expect her to be his target's main chick personally and professionally. Complications like that could spell doom for a hitter. You don't catch feels for anyone

Looking into Derryk's shocked eyes before putting a 9mm through his brain didn't bother Trigga in the least. The horror in Nyka's face, though, would be something he'd never forget.

A week ago, Trigga knew nothing about Derryk. All he had was the name, but a name is all Trigga needed to prepare for the job. Over the next few days, he learned everything he could about the man's life, his business, his routines, and especially his acquaintances. That's where he'd seen the name Nyka Sinclair. Yeah, Trigga knew her name, but he'd never seen her face until he met her at Dante's that night.

In one instant, Nyka transformed from potential loose end to his woman of destiny.

None of that had changed the rules of the game, though. Trigga had been given a job and that job was to murk Derryk Jones.

To set it up, Trigga studied the man's routine, staked out his club, even checked into a neighboring suite in the hotel Derryk holed up. The plan was simple: that night he would silently break into Derryk's suite, murk him, and then he and Wild would make it look as though a robber did the deed.

None of that took into account Trigga meeting Nyka, or Nyka showing up at Derryk's, or most importantly, Trigga seeing Derryk try to kill Nyka, the same way he'd seen his Papa try to kill his Mama when he was just a little boy.

And just like he had when he'd been a little boy, Trigga acted, and he acted decisively. Screw the future, he wouldn't allow Nyka to be sacrificed, even if it meant tempting fate.

"Ahh..ahh," Nyka huffed, trying to scramble away from him. Those beautiful eyes darted wildly, like an animal spooked. Trigga knew he had to be careful. People turned their most dangerous in situations like this, and another crazy turn was the last thing he needed right now.

With one hand he covered her mouth, and with the other Trigga put his finger to his lips. He hoped she got the meaning. He peeked up and down the hotel corridor. Forget taking care of witnesses, a good hitter avoided them in the first place.

Thankfully no one had peeked a nosy head out in response to the commotion of the door crashing. And since Trigga's piece always had a silencer, there was nothing to worry about on that front either.

"Damn babe, turn that TV down. Ain't no one trying to be deaf around here!" he yelled loud enough to echo through the corridor while staring into Nyka's bewildered eyes. If anyone *had* been listening to the commotion, a loud television was a flimsy enough explanation to keep them satisfied for a while. At least until Trigga could get control of this messed up situation and figure out what to do about the fine mound of curves now in his grip. She stared into him, confused, scared, and a little defiant, but at least she was smart enough not to make any noise. Her game face was indeed a turn-on, but he knew it was a front. She was the definition of a wild card at that very moment, and Trigga felt it as she trembled beneath his hands.

She gripped his wrist to remove his hand from her mouth. This was the moment, Trigga knew, when things either worked themselves out or went haywire. Keeping his hand over her mouth forever wasn't an option. He silently prayed for the best. After a moment, Trigga finally gave way, hoping for the best but ready to knock her out if need be.

They stared at each other for a few seconds, before Trigga slowly backed away to close the door. Nyka's eyes then found their way to Derryk's dead body. She reached for him and pulled back as she noticed Trigga walk back towards her. Nyka's eyes darted back and forth a few times before finally settling back on Trigga.

"You...you killed him," she whispered.

Trigga knelt to her level. "He was going to kill you, Ms. Nyka.

I've seen it before. You were in
the way of him getting what he
wanted."

He felt bad lying to her, but
the last thing Nyka needed to know
was what Trigga did for a living.

"But, you *killed* him!"

They didn't have time for
this, but he tried to humor her.
Nyka was clearly still in shock,
so he kept his voice low and calm.

"That's right. I killed him
before he killed you," he said,
nodding his head. She nodded in
agreement, slowly, but Trigga
noticed the look in her eyes.

Before he could blink, she bolted, heading straight towards the room phone. It didn't take much effort for Trigga to overtake her and secure her onto the floor, his hand back over her mouth.

They sat still, both heaving from exertion and excitement.

"You got it out of your system, lil Ma? Can I let you go now?"

Her eyes were fire, as she stared at him over her shoulder. But she nodded in agreement, and Trigga felt that she meant it.

He let her go again, and her doe eyes started to swell with tears.

He'd let her have her moment. Trigga looked around at the scene and made mental notes at the steps that needed completing. The plan was so off track it was almost funny.

The idea was to make the icing look drug related. Trigga knew Derryk had a side-business pushing powder through Dante's. And for every night the past week, at around two o'clock, one of his strippers, Honey, brought him the night's earnings before giving his dick a shine. They'd then smoke the night away. Before Honey arrived that night, Trigga would've bodied Derryk, Wild would bring up the rear to OD Honey enough to screw her memory, and the scene would've been made to look like a self-defense killing and robbery.

Knowing Honey, she would run and 'miraculously' find an extra 100k in her bank account to start a new life. It was the type of stunt Trigga and his cuz has pulled off half a dozen times since they were pups in Louisiana.

He looked down at the sobbing Nyka. There was time for a new plan. A *better* one. Nyka was right there, and all he had to do was pull out his piece and pull the trigger. Instead of one dead body there'd be two. A nice, simple murder-suicide from a crime of passion, as far as the 5-0 would be concerned.

Just murk the woman of your dreams. Simple as that. He'd been tasked to eventually do it anyway, before he knew who she was. Instead of Honey, he could make it look like Nyka killed Derryk and then herself. He reached into his pocket.

"Nyka," he said softly, knowing what needed to be done

She looked up, and he handed her a white handkerchief.

"I...I don't understand, Trigga. You killed him. How did you even know I was even here?"

Trigga reached down and helped her up. "I'll explain later. But now, I need to get you out of here."

He should've been surprised at how well she was taking the situation, but he wasn't. Nyka was a straight-out soldier-chick. Ride-or-die. Strong black women weren't a rarity, but didn't often run in his circles. So Nyka had instantly been attractive to him. He helped her up and guided her to the door, making sure to keep her head turned away from the dead body of her ex-fiancé.

Trigga made sure no one wandered the corridor before leading Nyka to his suite. He sat

her down on his bed, the intensity
of the last twenty minutes and her
body in her form-fitting dress
giving him inappropriate thoughts.
Nyka looked so vulnerable and
tired, and there was nothing
Trigga wanted more was to lay down
with her and take the worry away.

"You're a killer," she said,
her face betraying no depth
beneath the words.

"Yes, but a killer for you."

Who was he kidding? Of course,
at that moment, he'd killed
Derryk, not out of duty, but
because of a dream. He'd put a
bullet between a man's eyes for a

woman who was practically a
stranger.

And he'd damn well do it again
if given the chance.

"You're gonna have to trust
me, Ms. Nyka," he said, taking her
hands. "He *was* going to kill you.
There are some very powerful
people who want you out of the
way." And unfortunately for
Trigga, he worked for them.

She pulled her hands away, the
fire returned to her eyes. "I
think you need to explain to me
what's going on, Trigga. Who the
fuck are you, and why the fuck did
you just kill my man?"

Her man? Trigga clenched his lips and maintained his cool. "I'm someone who's trying to keep you safe, which *your man* definitely was not." He collected himself and picked up a small travel bag. "I need you to stay here, and I promise I'll explain when I get back. Deal?"

She nodded tentatively, and Trigga left for Derryk's suite. He took out a rag and some cleaner, and slipped on a pair of gloves from the bag. Methodically, he wiped the place clean of prints that would tie him or Nyka to the scene. He rubbed hard and vigorously, his motion betraying

the emotions he really didn't need
to be having at that moment.

This chick is something else.
He knew he shouldn't feel any sort
of way about Nyka's words,
considering she'd been in love
with Derryk for god knows how
long, and Trigga was just some cat
she'd met that night in a bar, but
Nyka's momentary coldness still
stung.

Get over yourself. Even though
he believed in Fate, and knew she
was the woman that had stalked his
dreams and would bless his life,
she knew nothing of it. In fact,
had she known, she really would be
freaking out. Trigga was a
spiritual man, but he knew no

everyone shared that conviction. To Nyka, his belief in destiny and fated love would probably sound downright crazy. Add to that the fact that he'd just killed his 'competition'.

Yeah, Trigga would have to get over the fact that she was mourning a lame negro who was ready to leave her for another woman with more money.

"You never knew what you had in Nyka, brotha, and you sure didn't deserve her," he said to the corpse as he dragged it to the bed, in order to cover it and delay its discovery.

Now that he thought about it, he couldn't help but wonder what Veeda had to do with any of this. Chick had always been her own woman, never even willing to be under Crux's thumb. But to step out on him like this for some busta and a club? Not even Veeda would go that far. Crux had to have known about it, right?

Yeah, there was something more going on. Something bigger. He could feel it.

Trapped in his own thoughts, Trigga didn't catch the presence of another person in the room until he sniffed the scent of a familiar cologne. He turned around to catch Wild surveying the room, his cocky grin barely covering the slight confusion on his face.

Trigga had been in the game long enough to recognize the tension in Wild's body. As he moved, Wild's right hand didn't stray far from the piece strapped on his side.

Trigga casually checked the clock. What was Wild even doing here so early? Yeah the thing with Derryk was supposed to be going down right now anyway, but Wild wasn't supposed to show his face until Honey finally showed hers. They'd planned it that way to minimize their time together, and decrease the likelihood of identification by any of the hotel's perceptive guests.

"Damn, nigga, you blew your nut early, didn't ya?" Wild said when he saw that Trigga had noticed him. Intuition told Trigga something was very wrong.

"Ay, man. Things got out of control. What are *you* doing here so early?" Trigga asked while he silently scolded himself for leaving his piece in his suite. He'd been so concerned about protecting Nyka that he was forgetting the basics.

"Just thought I'd hang out with my boy until it was time to work. Can't never learn too much

from the master, right?" Wild
lied, his high yellow skin red
with anticipation. "Say, where's
the chick?"

"Honey?"

"Nah, mayne. I already took
care of her. I'm talking about the
other one. This Derryk nigga's
main woman. What's her name, the
one you was fucking around with in
the club? Oh, yeah...Nyka."

They stared at each other for
a moment, feeling each other out.

"I don't know what you're
talking about. She got no reason
to be here," Trigga said,
pretending to wipe down some

surfaces so he could slyly close the distance between them.

Wild nodded his head, cocking a grin that showed most of his grill. "Little birdie I had keeping tabs on her told me otherwise.

"You sure you haven't seen her, killa?"

Trigga stayed silent as he inched closer. Wild's hand closed in on his piece.

"Too bad. I wanted to make this as clean as possible." Wild pulled out his gun and pointed it at Trigga's head. "Hope Veeda won't be too mad that I have a little fun first. All that voodoo shit you like, and you didn't even see this coming?"

"Trigga?" a voice said, coming from the door, momentarily drawing Wild's attention. *Dumb move, young buck.* In an instant, Trigga rammed into Wild's body, and things around them began to explode in a rain of gunfire.

CHAPTER EIGHT

NYKA

It didn't take long after
Trigga had left the room before
Nyka felt it all come crashing
down. Faking strength only went so
far. In a span of thirty minutes,
she'd tried to make up with
Derryk, found out Derryk wanted
her completely out of his life,
gotten beaten and probably almost
killed by the one-time love of her

life, and seen Derryk's brains splatter all over the room from a bullet by Trigga's gun.

Usually, suppressing tears came to Nyka naturally. Pushing those deep, hurtful feelings kept her sane growing up with the trifling Sista Treece. But the predicament she found herself in at that moment...shit, no way to keep the raindrops from flowing out her eyes.

She rubbed them with the back of her hands then realized that wouldn't be enough. On wobbly legs, she made her way to the bathroom and found some tissue.

She stared in the mirror. Her face looked back, all kinds of fucked up: raw, bruised, and smeared with runny makeup. It took a few swaths of tissue to clean herself, but wiping the pain and anguish away would take a hell of a lot more.

"Damn, girl. What have you gotten yourself into?" she said to herself. As she dried her hands, she knocked over a bottle of cologne, filling the bathroom with the spicy smell of island sexiness.

Trigga saved her, but she wasn't about to call him her black knight in shiny armor just yet. What the hell was he doing there anyway? Despite being grateful Trigga saved her from a world-class ass-whuppin...or worse...he gave her a weird vibe. Did he follow her? A stalker willing to kill? Shit couldn't get any crazier or realer than that.

She shook her head. Yeah, off-kilter described everything about Trigga, including the way he made her feel between her legs and in her heart. If she wanted to escape, she could. The police were only a telephone call away.

Yet, Nyka trusted Trigga. Crazy as it sounded, she'd never felt as safe around anyone in years.

But now that she'd wiped her face, cleared her eyes, and gotten control of her thoughts, she was ready for some answers, and Trigga damn well better provide them when he got back.

She made her way back to the bed and landed onto her back. "Ow!" she said as her head hit something hard. Pulling back the sheets, her heart stopped as she came face-to-face with the most god-awful ceramic mask she'd ever seen.

The fuck?, she thought to herself as she picked it up with shivering fingers. Nyka didn't have much experience with art, only a couple of classes in

college to round out her hours,
but she could tell the general
design was Caribbean. Painted
brown and black around the edges,
the mask's eerily lifelike
features only grew the more she
stared.

Nyka involuntarily dropped it
back onto the bed, and its blank
eyes stared back at her.

Hell. No. The shooting, the
killing, all the other bullshit
was bad enough. But this next
level horror shit was too much.

She needed to get away from
everything. From Trigga, from the
hotel, from Derryk's memory, and

most importantly, from her own dark thoughts and guilt.

The smart thing would be to call the police, but she had enough experience with the local 5-0 to know they weren't about shit. Besides, what was she going to tell them? That Derryk was killed by a sexy dark islander whom she'd just met, some mysterious killer she'd wanted to fuck 10 minutes after meeting at the club?

Something told her, no matter how much he was playing it off, that Trigga was no stranger to this sort of mess.

Trigger oozed danger, and the way nigga had acted after 'saving' her was entirely too calm for someone's first time.

Naw, even if Nyka called the cops, she doubted Trigga would hang around long enough to verify her story.

Hell, Nyka would probably end up being the one in jail. If anyone had a motive to kill muthafucking Derryk, it was her.

Besides, no matter how sideways she was beginning to feel about it, Trigga had saved her. She didn't want to get him into trouble, but common sense told her she needed to be as far as she could from him.

Trigga was a bad man. A dangerous man. And his sexiness and Nyka's weakness around him made that a lethal situation.

Nyka reached for her purse and into it, brushing her fingers against her Daddy's old revolver. She felt safer just touching it.

Yeah, it was time to get gone, and if anyone tried to stop her, they'd get it from Daddy's cold, blue steel.

She slipped on her heels and gave her eyes one final wipe.

Just as she was about to leave and haul ass, the sound of voices from Derryk's suite caught her attention. Trigga wasn't in there alone.

Forget it. Just leave. You made up your mind. GO!!! she told herself.

And she was about to, until she heard her name. Nyka.

Then suddenly, of course her feet did the opposite of what her brain demanded. One step, two steps...she made her way to Derryk's suite. One voice she recognized as Trigga's sexy one, the other...sort of familiar, but not really. She peeked her head

through the still-open door frame
and saw Trigga at the far end of
the room, and a second man, all
high yellow and skinny, his back
to her, just a few feet away.

The look on Trigga's face told
her something was wrong.

"Trigga?" she said,
immediately regretting it. The
young, yellow dude turned sharply,
a gun in his hand. Before Nyka
could react, Trigga was on him,
sending them both sprawling
towards Nyka, as a series of
gunshots exploded in the air.

Nyka screamed and fell
backwards into the hallway, her
hands covering her ears. In front

of her, the two men rolled on the floor, the younger man's gun evidently knocked away during the struggle.

"Muthafucker, get off me!" he screamed, as Trigga's fists connected with a couple of shots to his ribs.

The young buck quickly recovered, though, and slammed an elbow into Trigga's face. Trigga flew backwards, giving Trigga's foe a chance to finally roll over and get a bit of leverage. Before Trigga could recover, the kid sent a kick to his chest. A glass table exploded under Trigga's weight, and he let out a scream of pain.

By now, the hallway around Nyka had become a hotbed of activity. Curious, excited, and frightened heads peaked outdoors, and a couple of braver souls even came out, half naked and tentatively moving forward.

"The fuck is going on? Are you all right, miss?" an older, white guy from the far side of the corridor asked Nyka, whose hands were still shaking as she tried to protect her face.

When she didn't answer, the man took a step forward and Nyka, without thinking, reached into her purse and took out her gun.

"Don't come near me, any of
y'all!" she screamed, pointing the
revolver at anyone and everyone in
sight. More screams, as the group
of nosy busybodies made their way
back inside their suites with a
quickness.

Maybe it was crazy by Nyka,
but after everything she'd been
through, she didn't have it in her
to trust any stranger at that
point.

"Nyka!" Trigga screamed in
just enough time for Nyka to look
up and see the yellow nigga
standing. He'd found his gun.

At that moment, she met eyes
with Trigga, still on the floor in

the middle of broken glass. They were full of fear, much more so for her than for himself.

"Bitch, you don't know what to do with that," the boy said with cockiness, aiming at her with a grin on his face.

BLAM!

The asshole fell in a heap of pain as a chunk of his thigh exploded from Nyka's bullet.

"Fucking bitch!" he screamed, shakily bringing his gun back up to take another shot. Before Nyka had to take another shot, Trigga was back on his feet, over his foe, kicking him in the face. A couple headshots later, the young challenger was knocked out.

He looked up and saw Nyka's gun still held high, pointed right for his chest.

"I know you gonna break my heart, lil Ma, but I'd prefer it not be like this," he said with a bloody grin.

Nyka let herself ease in spite of herself, the gun lowering between her sprawled legs. "The fuck is going on, Trigga?"

"I promise, I'll explain later. But we got to get out of here, Nyka. I need you to trust me.

"You do trust me, right?" Trigga held out his hand in surrender.

Nyka shook her head at herself. She should've been long gone by now, but for some reason she was drawn to this man. At this point, she admitted to herself it was more than just physical attraction. More than chemistry. Something pulled her to him, kept her from walking away, made her go back to Derryk's suite when she didn't need to.

But trust him?

"Shit, I don't know who to trust at this point," she said, letting the events of the past hour crash her thoughts. "Trigga, you've been lying to me, haven't you?"

He couldn't hide it on his face. Of course he'd been lying to her. "We can talk about that later, but now, I need you to go back to my room and get ready to go."

"Go? Go where, Trigga?"

"Somewhere safe," he said, trying to sound reassuring in the middle of a sea of madness. He started to scoot in her direction, one hand still raised in surrender, the other reaching behind. "Until I can figure out what we do next."

"We? I know damn well you didn't say we!" Nyka came to her senses. "I'm not going anywhere with you! You just killed the love of my life, and because of you I just shot somebody, trying to protect your ass!"

"Nyka..."

"Hell no!" she started to raise her gun again. "I don't know who the fuck you think I am, but I ain't the..."

Before she could finish, he was on top of her in the hallway, one hand tightly clasping the back of her head while the other covered her nose and mouth. She struggled, barely noticing the sharp, stinging smell from his hand, until the world started to slow.

"Damn, Ms. Nyka, I didn't want to have to do this," he said, as world faded far, far away.

CHAPTER NINE

TRIGGA

Trigga couldn't front: it was the "love of my life" line Nyka yapped about that made his decision. Yeah, knocking her out with a face full of chemical had been a necessity, no doubt--baby girl was *this close* to flipping out, and the middle of that type of life-or-death situation was NOT the time for that mess. Trigga'd seen it in her eyes, could feel it from her body. That's the main reason he put her down.

But Nyka's words about Derryk sure made the deed a whole lot easier.

Trigga scolded himself for his jealousy. He'd met Nyka all of a few hours ago, so he had no right to be salty or to stake any sort of claim. But he'd known Nyka almost his entire life.

She lived in his dreams, stalked his thoughts, had stared at him from the mouth of fate. He knew it would all sound too poetic for someone as grounded like Nyka to understand, but Trigga knew it was true.

So much so that Trigga had compromised himself professionally to save her. Professionally and personally. Despite the blood between them, Crux would not be happy with Trigga for such a screw up. Being fam only went so far in the eyes of the Gulf Coast Mafia. Most important were results.

And the results of this job couldn't be described as anything but disastrous. Sure, Derryk was murked as he was supposed to, but Nyka was a loose end, Wild was bleeding all over the hotel floor, and the whole mess had gone down in anything but a quiet manner.

As Trigga dragged Nyka's unconscious body back into his

suite, he could hear the panic coming from the other rooms along the corridor. It a few minutes, the place would be swarming with hotel security, and soon after that, the police.

"Damn, damn!" he cursed to himself, something he rarely did since that day when he was a boy.

Since his Papa's death.

He quickly gathered his loot from under the bathroom sink, and sprayed the entire room with enough of his homemade cleaner to destroy any prints or taint DNA. Normally, he'd give everything a proper scrub-down, but time was not on his side.

He checked his watch. Luckily, he and Wild had a hook-up with hotel security, and paid for the cameras to be down for a window of ten minutes. That should've been enough time, but of course that was before everything went crazy.

Now time was running out.

Trigga was thankful he had even that much time, though. Not only that, but the hook-up had done even more: the elevators were disabled, and the service stair entrances were blocked except for the floor they were on. A well-planned hit, as was always the case with Trigga, that had gone left before it had even begun. He and Wild should've been long gone by now..

And speaking of Wild, what was that about? Just a case of a young buck trying to step up at the wrong time, seizing an opportunity to move up in the ranks, or was there something more behind it?

Trigga remembered the mention of Veeda's name. Veeda...

Trigga snapped out of it. There'd be time to analyze the situation later, but now he had to get himself and Nyka out of there and somewhere safe. Normally, there'd be a safe house set up for such an event, but that was out of the question, considering he hadn't had the chance to set one up. There'd been no need. Simple job that shouldn't have had any complications. *Damn*.

But Trigga had an idea.

Almost done, he frantically searched the bed for the last thing he needed. The mask. It wasn't where he'd have left it, meaning Nyka must've discovered it.

Yet another strike against him in her eyes. The dream mask looked scary, even to him after all these years. No telling what crazy thoughts it gave Nyka about him.

Soon he'd explain it to her. If she really was the woman he

believed, he'd explain everything to her and she'd understand. She had to, right?

He shoved the mask in his bag, and decided to worry about it later like everything else.

He then hoisted Nyka's fine self over his shoulder, giving that behind a slap for good measure, and started out the door.

Leaving the room, he heard a moaning from the room next door. Wild must be coming to.

One bullet would put this dumb buck out of his misery. But killing the crazy mutha would be a step too far, considering he was Veeda's nephew, and by extension

Crux's, and that was a hornet's
nest he didn't need to stir up.
But he couldn't just leave him.
That was another loose end he
needed to clip.

"The wound isn't that bad,
Wild," Trigga yelled in Wild's
general direction. "You got about
a minute to get up before this
whole thing starts swarming!"

"Imma kill you, muthafucker!
You hear me, you DEAD!" the boy
responded, pissed at having a
chunk of his leg blown to pieces.
Yet another reason to get Nyka
away from that mess: Wild might
not be smartest or the most
professional, but he was a vicious
little mutt, and he damn sure

would be coming after Nyka for revenge.

He could already hear the loud stomping of security from the main staircase. Thinking quickly, he pulled the fire alarm, and in seconds the corridor filled with people. They pushed their way into the main staircase, overwhelming the incoming security personnel.

No one seemingly noticed him and Nyka's limp body make their away in the other direction.

"Ms. Nyka, you stacked pretty well, 'cause you sure weigh more than you look," he joked to himself. To his surprise, Nyka groaned and weakly punched his

back in response. Trigga admired
her spirit. A normal bird would've
been out cold from the amount of
knockout stuff he gave her, but
this one was fighting it with
everything she had.

Trigga kicked open the service
staircase and started his trek
down, floor by floor, each landing
entrance blocked, just as they
were meant to be. He stopped at
the one on the second floor and
removed the blockage.

Security and the police would
be expecting any troublemakers to
exit on the first floor.

But Trigga was no rookie, and
he sure as heck was no fool.

Crashing into the second floor, he quickly made his way down the surprisingly empty main corridor, took a left, then another left, and found himself at the end of a dimmest hallway branch and in front of a door that said 'Employees Only'. He turned the knob and entered the part supply room/part lounge.

Just as he'd paid for, no one was in the room, so there'd at least be no loose ends there.

At the far end of the room stood another unmarked door that he kicked open. He made his way down the dimly lit, narrow staircase until they reached the door at the bottom.

When he opened it, he was somewhat surprised by the fresh night air and the quietness. After the mess-ups of the past hour, he half expected the back lot of the hotel to already be filled with po-po's ready to let their trigger fingers go wild.

But just as originally planned, his tan Lexus GS sat waiting for him for a quick getaway. Carefully, he laid Nyka in the front seat, buckled her, and took off, driving past a platoon of cop cars traveling in the direction towards the hotel murder scene.

Letting out a sigh of relief, Trigga flicked the satellite radio on and scrolled for some hip-hop. The sounds of Rich Homey Quan's *Most* filled the cabin and he let himself get lost in the beat.

"MMEERRRGGGKKK"

Trigga heard Nyka mumble as if she were in a dream. She slowly shook her head from side-to-side, seemingly fighting whatever weighed her down in her current state.

"MMEEERRRRYYKK"

More mumbling. Trigga reached over to the passenger seat and brushed his hand across the side of her face. It felt smooth and soft, so much so he was tempted to keep touching her past her neck.

Even though he shouldn't have, he
couldn't help but side-eye her
ample cleavage.

Stop it, Trigga, he told
himself.

Trigga grinned. Back in his
right frame of mind, he picked up
his phone and dialed the one
number he was dreading.

After a few rings, a deep
voice boomed through the phone's
speaker.

"Sup, Killer? I been waiting
for your call." Crux's voice
vibrated through the voice, a hint
of a Haitian accent present to
give away his heritage.

"Sup, cuz?" Trigga responded, trying to sound as calm as possible.

"Biz taken care of?"

"The main biz, yeah, but not without some static in the wire," Trigga said, using the code they'd come up with when they were kids.

Crux sighed with the frustration of a man not used to hearing about failure, especially not from his number one cuz. "When can you get to me on the hotline?"

"Gimme til the morning. I need some sleep to get my mind straight."

"Bet. Where's High Yella?" Crux asked, using their code for Wild.

"Part of the problem, Cuz. I'm gon' have to figure out a solution."

"Alright. Out." Crux ended the call abruptly. Trigga knew his cuz, and that he seethed with anger right now. Trigga would figure out a way to make things right, but his main concern was Nyka. He looked back over in her direction, and she still moved her head from side to side. With the car now quiet, he listed more intently to her mumbling.

"MMMDerrryk. MMMMsssooo sorry."

Trigga restrained himself from hitting the steering wheel. That dead negro was getting on his very last nerve.

CHAPTER TEN

WILD

Wild cursed at Trigga for
another few seconds before
realizing he'd already made his

escape. The fire alarm screamed in his ears, pissing him off even more, but at least it would buy him some time.

He had to get out of there, and that shit had to happen with a quickness.

Wild hollered in agony as he got to his feet. He mugged his wound and it made him want to hurl. Even though he was a hitter-in-training, blood creeped him the fuck out.

His own blood, anyway. It oozed from the open gash and through his Ricky Straight jeans, turning its dark blue color black.

Fuck!

It wasn't anywhere near as deep as the pain initially led him to believe, but the shit still hurt nevertheless. He was going to kill that Nyka bitch when he caught up with her, right after he finished Trigga's chicken-leg eating ass. He'd never liked the punk-ass nigga anyway, and he'd be damned if he'd let Trigga cost him his stripes with Crux.

And fuck if he was going to disappoint Veeda. Woman might have the outward appearance of calmness, but she was mad crazy when it came to getting her way.

When it came to Wild, Veeda always got her way. Or else.

Nah, he had to get this shit together NOW.

While the fire alarm would slow the hotel thugs and the po-po's, it wouldn't for very long. And despite what that punk-ass Trigga though, Wild didn't like sloppiness. No, he didn't meticulously carry around homemade chemicals and a bag of fake IDs, but he knew enough about enough to get by.

Hopping over to the room's desk, he took a few scraps of stationary, threw them in the trash, got his lighter, and lit that bitch. He then held up the trash basket near the ceiling until the sprinklers came on.

There. Instant cleanup for his blood.

He rolled up his pant leg enough to catch any dripping blood and began to haul ass out the hallway.

"Hold it right there!" a fat-ass squaw in a cheap suit yelled from the end of the hall, with an equally fat partner following close behind. Indian security.

"Mane, fuck y'all," Wild yelled as he sent a torrent of bullet flying in their direction, hitting both of the fuckers right in the leg. They yelled in pain.

Good. Now they knew how he felt.

Shooting Indians hadn't been a part of the plan, but neither had mowing down Trigga. Until it was. Plans change, and a nigga gotta adapt.

Wild limped his way into the tiny service stairway and secured it behind him with one of the sleeves of his Versace tee. He took the other sleeve and wrapped it around his leg wound, nice and tight.

Nah, Wild didn't like messing with blood, but that didn't mean he didn't know how. Growing up with a sister who cut herself and a junkie momma had taught Wild a lot of shit people didn't know about.

He might be crazy, but he sure as fuck wasn't stupid.

With the bleeding somewhat under control, Wild gingerly made his way down the stairs until he got to the second floor. From there, he made his way to the secret employee's exit and into the parking lot.

Luckily, all the cop cars were on the other side of the building. Not that Philadelphia had much in the way of cops anyway. The local cops were there now, and it would probably take another five minutes for the county pigs to make an entrance.

He didn't see Trigga's Lexus. Not that he expected to, but it would've felt good to put some holes in that bitch out of frustration.

Wild chirped his Audi and eased himself into the driver's side leather seat.

"God damn, that feels good," he said, finally able to take pressure off his leg. Without hesitation, he started the car and put in drive, lights off, easily avoiding the notice of the cops and residents waiting around in the parking lot.

Before getting back on the main highway, he wanted to stop at

a fast food joint and get
something to eat, but thought
better of it. He didn't need his
face to be seen any more than it
already had.

Besides, Wild damn well knew
he was stalling for time. He'd
fucked up, and no amount of side
stops would change that. He needed
to call Veeda and give her the
situation.

Just as he had the thought,
his phone lit up.

Goddamn.

"Aunt Vee, this ain't the
time," he said through the car's
bluetooth.

"Is that so, baby boy?" Veeda said, her voice as smooth and unwavering as ever. It always gave Wild the chills in a way no other woman's had. "I'm looking at my watch, and this seems to be perfect time.

"Right about now, you should be giving me good news about the special job I gave you. Where's my good news?"

Wild sucked in his breath and hesitated, wondering how much info she absolutely needed to have right now.

"Vee, don't worry about it. Dat nigga Derryk..."

"I know all about Derryk being dead. So I should warn you, before you open that mouth any more, Theodore," she sternly interrupted, using his real name as a power play, "and give me some lies or half-truths, just know that I know a few little birdies at the hotel. You need to give me the fucking rundown right now."

Shit.

"Look, Derryk's dead, but that nigga Trigga went off the script. That hoe he was with at the club fucked him up in the head."

She gave a heavy sigh. "By 'that hoe', I assume you mean the woman Derryk was supposed to kill?"

"Yeah, Ma. None of that shit went the way it was supposed to. Instead of fucking her up and taking care of loose ends, Trigga fell for the pussy like a little bitch. Messed up any chance I had to ice him."

"And you couldn't handle them both? That what you saying?"

"Yeah." At that moment, Wild felt lower than a man. Admitting failure to Veeda killed him, considering how much she depended on him. She'd practically raised him. Nurtured him. Taught him to be a man in ways he wouldn't have otherwise.

"You are going to take care of this, aren't you? I got big plans for us. You my main nigga, and I need to know you're worthy of being by my side when I take what's mine."

"Don't worry about that shit, Veeda. I just need to get stitched up and I'll track that fool and his bitch down."

"Are you hurt?" she asked, the concern in her voice putting Wild at easy a bit.

"Just a flesh wound. I'll shake it off."

"Do you need me to look at it? I can make it feel better..." she said, her words making Wild feel all sorts of ways he didn't need to. Veeda had that way about her. He knew her well enough to know that she was an expert at getting cats to do whatever she wanted. Right now, though, he needed no extra motivation.

"Nah, it's cool. Imma stop by that squaw chick's house and get squared up. She's been the one sourcing me info down here, and she can help me take care of Trigga and his."

"Mmm," Veeda said after a moment of silence, making Wild anxious on top of everything else.

"Just make sure you're keeping your head in the game while you're with your *source*. Wouldn't want you ending up like Trigga."

"Aye," Wild said, happy they were finally ending the call. He didn't like the way Veeda pulled his strings. She was an ambitious chick, and treated Wild as nothing more than an asset most of the time.

This plan of hers to take out Trigga? All hers on the fly. And Wild still didn't know why. Hell, despite Veeda saying otherwise, he was beginning to wonder if even Crux even knew what the fuck was going on.

Wild bit his lip and shook his head. Enough with whining. He wanted to be a front line soldier in the GCM, and this was his chance. However Veeda's plan played out, he'd be by her side, and in the end, they'd be on the winning team.

No doubt.

He pressed a button on the dashboard to dial his pretty little source. She picked up the phone, and before she could say a word, he let her know what's up.

"I need some stitches and some pussy. Be ready in ten."

CHAPTER ELEVEN

VEEDA

Veeda lightly laughed as she applied a layer of gloss and popped her lips. It amused her that men could be so goddamn trifling. Love them, save them, stand by them, give them your heart...none of it really matter. Only one thing ever came first, in the end.

New pussy over loyalty. Always the same damn song.

It didn't even bother her anymore that the men in her life exemplified this in the worst way. Thinking with their dicks and fixing mistakes with their guns.

The weapons of a dumb lifestyle.

But Veeda knew what was what. She'd been around guns a long time, and around dicks even longer. Both worked the same. It took no more effort to sway a trigger-happy nigga than a horny one. Whisper in his ear, caress his steel, and a man would shoot in any direction you ask him to.

Do it enough times, and he'd beg for it.

It had worked on her Daddy, it had worked on her first pimp, then Crux, and now even Wild.

Let the little yellow nigga have his fun. In the end, he'd always come back home to Aunt Veeda.

She always did it best.

Veeda stepped out of her BMW into the flashing police lights of the hotel parking lot. Dressed in a zipper bustier and Baby Phat jeans, she immediately drew attention from the crowd. Especially the men.

Her heels clicked the pavement as she made her way to the police tape. An officer gave her a quick look up and down, curious at the pretty thing coming his way, before finally holding up his hand for her to stop.

"Ma'am, we're asking everyone already outside to stay outside for the time being. Once everything's secure..."

"Chief Jordan is expecting me, Officer. If you wouldn't mind contacting him? Tell him Veeda St. Croix is here." Veeda said confidently, yet with enough friendliness to keep him off-guard.

The officer nodded, then turned to the side, his eyes never really leaving Veeda's body, and spoke into his shoulder radio. When the response finally came, he told Veeda wait right there in front of him.

"Whatever you say." Veeda smiled, eliciting a small grin from the officer.

No, Veeda had never needed a gun to get what she wanted. And soon, she wouldn't need anyone's dick either to control her fate.

Chief Jordan stomped through the hotel exit, his eyes darting from side to side until they squared on Veeda. He was a middle aged negro, sweaty and dark, and of course married and unsatisfied with that fact. He didn't have much to offer her except access, which he gladly gave in exchange for a few greasy minutes of her time.

It was a perfectly fair trade in her book. Too bad he didn't realize that business with Veeda meant a commitment above and beyond a simple fuck.

"You can go," he told the young officer, who proceeded to awkwardly nod at Veeda before going away. "Veeda, you can't be here right now. This is a crime scene..."

"I know what this is, Jeffrey. That's why I need you to escort me to where Derryk Jones died."

Jordan looked at her stupidly. He glanced around to make sure no one else could hear their conversation. "And how the fuck do you know about Derryk Jones?

Veeda gave him a look of bemusement. "Don't fucking worry how I know about your crime scene and your victim. Just get me in that hotel and into Derryk Jones' suite. Everything else, you shouldn't worry your precious little self about." She patted his face, feeling a bit irritated by his not getting with the program.

The fat fuck gave her another stupid look, this time pissing Veeda off. "Veeda, you might think you some big, bad bitch from the Coast, but fuck you think you're going to tell me what to do in my town, at my crime scene.

"Your pussy might be tight, but not even it has jurisdiction around here."

She chuckled. "You'd be surprised at the jurisdiction under my pussy's control, you fat fuck," she said, immediately enraging him. "And maybe you think you're dealing with one of these dumb country chicks, but I ain't the one. This is an Indian establishment on Indian land, and ultimate authority is federal, not local. You're here as a courtesy until the real dicks show up.

"But until then, the Natives have the real power, and if you'll be so nice as to check with the ones calling the shots, you'll find that I've been given permission to do whatever the fuck I want when I want to."

Jordan balled his fist as if to make a motion, but he knew better. She might've been pussy, but she was well-connected pussy, and he knew that even without her having to tell him about Crux. Instead of saying any more dumb shit, he turned his back and made a call.

Veeda remained patient. A minute later, with Jordan's pride shrunk to the size of that sad thing he called a dick, he led Veeda past the crime scene tape and up the elevator.

On the way, he gave a summary of what had gone down, from Derryk Jones' apparent murder, to the shootout that occurred shortly later between unidentified assailants. One thing for some dumb muthafucker to be killed in a Choctaw-owned hotel, but for a couple of Choctaws to be shot on the scene? There would be serious repercussions for that.

Veeda quietly seethed as he continued. Wild damn well needed to re-earn her trust after a fuck-up of this magnitude. Maybe had things gone sideways in the process of Wild actually accomplishing his mission she could be more forgiving, but neither Nyka or, most importantly, Trigga, got what was coming to them.

That shit could not stand.

Keeping Crux off her back during this affair had taken a monumental effort already. But she'd have to think fast to explain all of this.

No telling how much Trigga had already opened his mouth about to him. If not for the fact of Trigga

fucking up himself, she'd be a
dead woman walking.

Luckily, Trigga falling in
love with a country bitch would
buy her some time.

They arrived at Derryk's
suite, where a small group of cops
and techs continued to work.

"Tell them to leave, Chief."

"What?"

"I'm not going to say it
again." She looked him squarely in
the eyes. Jordan reluctantly gave
the order, and everyone got out,
confused and curious as to who
really called the shots.

"That goes for you too," she said, not looking at him while stepping through the doorway.

Jordan made a faint sound as if he wanted to speak, then shut his trap and turned on his heels.

Veeda looked around at the mayhem. Perfect example of when ghetto meets penthouse. She walked across the wet floor to a box of examiner gloves, taking a pair and putting them on.

She carefully removed her earrings and placed them in her pocket. She secured any other loose items on her body. Then she got to the job at hand

She began to comb the immediate area. Bullets and broken glass. A couple of discarded Black N Milds. An unopened rubber.

Messiness from a messy nigga.

But it didn't take long before she found the soggy remains of what she'd set out to find. She picked up the draft of the transfer of ownership paperwork and combed through the pages.

No signature where Nyka's should've been. Damn. Veeda had hoped she'd be lucky and that Derryk would've gotten the bitch to sign first.

Guess Derryk wasn't quite the man he thought he was.

She rolled the sheets and stuffed them in her back pocket. A bottle of brandy lay undisturbed on a table nearby, so Veeda poured herself a glass to calm her nerves.

The level of incompetence surrounding this shit astounded her. She knew she needed to point a finger at herself on that too. Sloppiness is a bitch's worst enemy.

But Veeda learned quick. Those same mistakes wouldn't happen again.

She finished her glass, and began the walk to the sleeping quarter of the suite. She stepped over debris and the trail of blood until she stood at the bed, Derryk's corpse splayed in a pool of red.

She sat next time him and touched his face.

"Nothing personal, babe. You know how business goes," she whispered to him. And that was one of the things she admired about him, that he did understand business was cruel. Even though he'd been nothing more than a means to an end, she couldn't help but respect his hunger and drive. Instead of settling for the mediocrity of a somewhat-successful business and a happy wife at home, Derryk wanted greatness.

To be boss.

Nigga had stepped up and practically volunteered to kill the woman he wanted to make vows to, just so he could make something better for himself in the world.

And he did because Veeda wanted it so.

She ran a finger down his cold nose. Dedication. Loyalty. Her fingers stopped at his lips. And wasn't bad at eating the pussy either.

In other life, maybe he could've been something more. But not in this one.

After paying her respects, she gave the entire place a good combing over, discarding anything that would associate Derryk with her or anyone on the Gulf Coast. Satisfied the room was clean, she returned to Derryk's body and patted down his robe.

She reached into his pocket and took out his phone. She'd take it with her, but curiosity made her stroll through the contacts, until she came to Nyka.

She wondered...

Unlike Wild, Trigga usually stayed on his game. There was no way he'd answer any calls on his own phone from anyone but Crux, and knowing him, he'd be hesitant to do even that. And he sure as hell wouldn't let Nyka answer hers.

Paranoid Haitian niggas.

But maybe he wouldn't be on his game. She dialed Nyka's number and let it ring.

Nothing.

She had an idea. 'NYK, IM STILL ALVE. ANSWR ME!!!' She sent the text and gave it a minute.

She then dialed the number again and, 'lo and behold, the line picked up. There was silence, but she knew who was on the other end.

"Hello Trigga. I knew curiosity would get the best of you."

More silence, and then, "You tried to kill me, Veeda."

Trigga's angry voice made her wet. "Last time you sounded so mad, you nearly blew my back out with that thick snake. Should I be getting ready for that big ol' hook again?"

"Veeda, I don't know what kind of game you're playing, but when Crux finds out..."

"He's going to do what? Spank me? Bust my face up? Been there, done that. No matter what, that nigga trust me. I'm not so sure about you after tonight."

Silence. "What do you want, Veeda?"

"I don't know what kind of spell that little peas-and-grit bitch put on you, but you can have her. After I have her signature. You weren't supposed to kill Derryk until after he got her to sign over her club share and her pledge not to make any trouble afterwards."

Trigga gave a tired laugh. "You expect me to believe that if you get her signature and a promise, you won't try to kill her anymore."

"Cross my heart."

"Yeah, lemme think about that and I'll get back to you," he said sarcastically. "None of that explains why you little boy toy tried to murk me."

"He got a little too enthusiastic, that's all, baby," she lied. "You know how niggas are when they're trying to come up."

"I know how women are too, in that situation. The answer is no."

Veeda sighed, not at all surprised. She didn't expect Trigga to fall for her trap, but he'd let her unwittingly know how far he was willing to go for Nyka.

"Don't say I didn't give you a chance."

With that, Trigga hung up on her, and Veeda knew what had to be done. By now, he'd probably taken the battery out of the phone, so tracking them that way would be impossible. But he couldn't be very far, and he was off his game.

She stuck Derryk's phone in her pocket, gave him a last kiss, and proceeded to leave. As she passed Jordan on her way to the lobby, she made sure she he had a good look at the blood-stained paperwork sticking out of the back of her pants. She gave him a wicked grin, daring him to say shit about her removing shit from a crime scene.

He didn't, and she exited into the night, ready to take what was hers by any means necessary.

CHAPTER TWELVE

CRUX

Growing up eating his momma's homemade legim and yams had made Crux a big man. Being second generation Haitian refugee had made him hard. And running the fastest rising mafia in the entire Southeast had made him a man with an appetite for the most life had to offer.

"Ohhhh, Papi, right there! Dat dick so biggggg!!!"

And right now, his appetite craved something spicy. And there wasn't anything spicier than some good Cuban pussy riding his dick.

"Keep that shit open, goddamn," he barked at the bitch, not really feeling her silly need to tighten her thighs as he rode her.

He was a big man with a big need. He wanted that pussy wide.

He smacked her fat ass, before forcefully grabbing her cheeks and spreading them as far as possible. To Henrietta's credit, she never missed a beat, continuing to meet and then anticipate his pumps.

In fact, he could tell she was loving that shit. Pretending to resist while pleasing that dick. He couldn't lie, it stroked a nigga's ego to feel her so wet.

"Fuck yea. You know how Papi likes it, don't you?"

"Nice and hot."

Her thick ass had been the first thing he'd noticed when he interviewed her. And she knew he noticed, and winked in response. It gave her a leg up on the competition to know he could get her legs up in the air when it was time. Despite Veeda's reservations, he hired her the next day.

And started fucking her a couple days later.

Don't get it twisted. Smart business and the money came first. He'd never do anything to weaken his position and the flow of green, even if it meant good pussy. Henrietta's administrative game was on point, and her contacts within the Cuban cartel had come in handy more than once.

Business before pleasure was the type of thinking that'd makes you a success. Being able to mix business and pleasure successfully is what puts you on top.

Crux had mastered the art of only fucking pussy that made him stronger.

He kept Henrietta bent over his office desk and wrapped her long hair around his fist. He pulled with one hand, evoking a raspy scream from her throat. With his other hand, he slipped a finger in her ass. She buckled wildly like a stallion, both holes gripping Crux for dear life.

"Goddamn, I'm about to cum!" he yelled, pulling out to bust a load on her red backside.

She turned over and licked his dick clean, before zipping him up and adjusting his Gucci suit like a good assistant.

Crux checked himself in the mirror. "Good. Now get me some breakfast!"

"Yes, Mr. St. Croix," Henrietta replied, limping out of his office.

Crux checked his phone again and cursed. Still nothing more from his cuz Trigga on that business, and it started to bother him. What the fuck was taking so long? And why hadn't shit gone right in the first place? It wasn't like Trigga to mess up a hit anyway, but not to fix that shit with a quickness? And then leave his fam in the cold wondering what was up?

That shit couldn't fly.

If that wasn't bad enough, Veeda didn't answer her shit, either. Not that that was anything new, but disrespect was disrespect. It had been her idea to let Wild's dumb ass tag along with Trigga to get a feel for the work, but from what little his cuz had communicated, Wild was a part of the problem, not the solution. She needed to answer for that shit.

Crux hated dumb decision and incompetence.

He couldn't blame anyone but himself. His Papa had taught him to never use a bullet when a blade would do, and sending so many people to take care of one simple acquisition had struck him as dumb from the very beginning.

But for the Gulf Coast Mafia to become a true force, it needed to get a foothold in the Indian casino racket. And for that to happen, it needed a stronghold in the area. What better way than to take Dante's Inferno, a club with hot word-of-mouth and guaranteed business, which just so happened would be built on land right outside a Choctaw reservation, next to a thriving casino?

It was perfect.

And to make it happen? The two owners--some nigga named Jones and his bitch--had to give it up willingly or by force. Didn't matter which.

Couldn't have been simpler.

Because of Veeda's special talent with persuading niggas of shit they don't even know they want, he'd let her take point. Once she finished, Trigga would clean up. No overlap. Trigga didn't even have to know Veeda was there.

In fact, he preferred it that way. Trigga and Veeda clashed. He didn't know why, but he suspected.

Anyway, Crux had come up with a good plan.

But shit never goes the way it's supposed to, does it?

He needed to calm down. His plush Armani Xavira chair groaned as he eased into it and stared out the wall-to-wall window into the morning scene. His Daddy and the rest of his OGs could've only dreamed of this when they migrated from Haiti, with only a few hundred dollars, a bag of knives, and a viciousness to be something better.

Crux closed his eyes, took a few breaths, and tried Veeda's phone again. Bitch damn well had better pick u...

"Hello Horatio," she purred, even though she damn well knew Crux would be hot from her avoiding his calls. "I was just about to call you."

"Don't even try that shit, V. Answer the fucking phone when you supposed to," he snapped, feeling his heat rising again.

"Baby, don't be like that. I figured I'd let you get your morning workout before talking to you. I know how grumpy you get without it. Speaking of which, how is Henrietta?"

Crux rolled his eyes. Veeda loved trying him, but he had something for her, alright. Only one of them wore the dick in that marriage.

"And how's that bitch-ass nephew of yours? I heard he's causing trouble, as usual. Maybe he ain't ready to let go of your tits just yet."

Veeda didn't say anything for a moment, and neither did Crux. Veeda had always been an asset to the GCM, and not that bad of a wife when she wanted. But her thirst was getting the better of her, and her soft spot for that sorry nephew of hers was going to be their undoing.

"Maybe you need to get your fact straight, Baby. It wasn't my fam who fucked shit up last night."

He had a hard time believing that, but had to admit his curiosity was piqued. "Oh really? Enlighten me."

"You cousin fell in love with a mark, Horatio. And when Wild came by to do clean up, he shot him and escaped with the his new love."

Crux let the words sink in. "You're lying."

Veeda blew a sympathetic sigh. "Now baby, you know better than that. From the way Wild tells it, it was first sight with Trigga. Or maybe that's what the coffee grinds was telling him."

Coffee grinds? Crux clenched his lips. He and Trigga were first cousins, and grew up as brothers in Haiti Town among all the traditions and superstitions of the home island. Both were second gen Haitian killers, and both grew up in the game and its hard lessons. But while Crux's only motive concerned the money, Trigga had another side.

Hanging around old priestesses and dancing voodoo folk made him believe stuff Crux couldn't get down with. And while Trigga was hardcore, Crux's right hand hitter, he gave too much importance to this destiny and fate stuff.

But Crux never believed it would come before family business.

"I can't believe that, V."

"Can't, or won't? I think you know the truth, Horatio. You talk about me and weak spots, but that nigga has always been yours."

He pinched the bridge of his nose. Fuck, she was right. "Whatever, man. I'll take care of cuz. If he's off in the head, I got him worked out. All I need to know if we can get that paperwork straight."

"Let me and Wild take care of that. And if Trigga gets in the way, do you give us the go to take care of him too?"

Crux hesitated, looking at the chain of luxury cars pulling up downstairs. His potential Choctaw business partners from Philadelphia. This whole operation should've been done by now. He didn't know jack shit about the reds, and he feared no man on this earth, but the Indians he'd met were no joke. Things could get needlessly complicated if the situation didn't rectify itself. Immediately. They'd already spent significant time, money, and influence to get the ball rolling on their end, contingent on Crux actually owning Dante's Inferno and the land surrounding it.

"He's fam, but if he gets in the way of business..." Crux closed his eyes. "If it comes to that, you don't do shit unless I give the say so, understand, V?"

"Of course, Baby. You're the boss," she said, sending a smooch through the phone before handing up.

Crux threw the phone onto his desk. Killing his own cuz? Nah, it would never come to that, but he needed all his subordinates, including Veeda, to think that he could.

But actually ending Trigga? No way would Trigga push him to that extreme. No goddamn voodoo shit could drive him that far to the left. Right?

Crux stood, looking out his oversized windows into the beautiful world outside. He wished he could know what his Daddy would do in his situation, but he had the next best thing. As frustrating as dealing with Veeda could be, his mother was so much worse.

"Where's my goddamn breakfast, Henrietta?" he yelled, his appetite suddenly whet once again.

CHAPTER THIRTEEN

NYKA

His eyes, his smile, his stride, his kiss--everything about

Derryk appeared so vivid, so real, but blurry like Sunday morning. His voice, his breath, his temper, his hands--the image of him turned cruel, and she felt him striking her face. He stood above her, strangling her, his love now nothing but greed.

Just before it all turned black for her, his face exploded, a hole slicing through its center. High above Nyka, her savior reached out for his, the ugliest fucking mask for a face she'd ever seen.

Nyka screamed herself awake.

It was all a goddamn dream, she thought to herself. That

couldn't have been real. No way
had she been involved in the
events of she kept dreaming about.
That reservation weed Red gave her
delivered something fierce.

She was soaked in sweat to her
drawers.

MMPHHH!!!

Nyka had no choice but to
acknowledge the truth of her
situation when she tried to wipe
her face. Her hands were bound.
She tried to scream. Her mouth
taped shut.

She tugged as hard as could
against the bedpost. She wasn't
even in her own goddamn bed. It
took a hot minute before her eyes

completely adjusted to the surroundings. Clothes sat here and there. A group of balled up ones sat on a table.

Worst of all, the entire place smelled like thot.

"Good morning, Ms. Nyka. I was hoping I'd get back before you woke up," a voice said from the side. Trigga walked into the bedroom, his sexy grin on full display. In his hands he carried a McDonald's bag. "I got you breakfast."

Nyka let out a muffled scream and bucked wild against her restraints. She needed something to be free: her mouth or her arms.

It didn't even matter which, as long as she could either knock the shit out of Trigga with her fists or curse his island ass out until he was back across the ocean.

"No need to be profane, Ms. Nyka," he teased her, infuriating a sister even more. "I need you to bring it down a level."

She didn't know who this nigga thought he was, but telling her what to do wasn't gonna fly.

Trigga laid the food on the bed and sat next to her. He grabbed her leg to calm her, his firm grip slowly going soft as he rubbed her thigh up and down.

In spite of herself, Nyka softened. Of all of the weak spots he could discover, he had to find her pussy-wetter. The look on his face let her know that her sudden compliance didn't escape his notice. He concentrated on the spot he'd accidental found, rubbing it slowly back and forth with his fingertips, reveling in the smoothness and the reaction she tried to hide.

She didn't want to be that easy, but Trigga was making it easy to be that way. She wanted to hate this nigga who'd cause so much drama in her life in so little time, but for some reason she didn't have it in her.

He gave her a wicked grin, those perfect teeth framed by his perfectly cut mouth.

"Okay, now that I got your attention, let's get on the same page," he started, digging into her with them deep brown eyes. "First of all, I'm not your enemy. You understand that, right?"

Nyka didn't know how to answer, so she didn't.

"Ok, lil Ma, let's go about this another way. Wasn't I there to keep you from shooting Derryk at Dante's?"

She nodded.

"And wasn't I there to keep Derryk from killing you in his hotel room?"

She nodded.

"And didn't I get us out safely before Wild could kill us both?"

She reluctantly nodded.

"So, lemme ask you again, Nyka. Do you trust me?"

She thought about it for a sec. Everything he was saying rang true. Even though Nyka wasn't the type to hand out trust, she couldn't help but admit that Trigga had done a lot to earn some partial trust.

Besides, she didn't exactly have a choice.

He pulled the tape from her mouth.

"Trigga, did you fucking drug me?" she asked. He gave her a half smile.

"I had to do it for your own good, Ms. Nyka. Don't worry, I was a gentleman the entire time. Although," he said, eying her up and down like an animal with juicy prey "seeing you tied up like this tempted me many, many times through the night."

She twisted her lips and mockingly blew her lips at the idea. She should've minded the idea, but didn't. "You wouldn't have known what to do with this, anyway."

Trigga laughed, then took out a knife and switched the blade. Nyka jumped. Moving faster than the eye, he cut the bindings from her hands. Nyka rubbed her hands cautiously. It was crazy, the blade hadn't even touched her during the entire process.

"So on top of everything else, you're good with a knife, huh?"

"My Daddy was Haitian, so it's in my blood." He handed her the bag. "Pancakes. I know we haven't had breakfast together before, but something tells me you could eat the hell out of some flapjacks."

"Nigga please," she said, rolling her eyes. He wasn't even close to being wrong, though. She was a hoe for some mickey D's pancakes.

Damn, was she hungry. She tore through the bag and chomped on the deliciousness. Trigga looked on intently, sipping a cup of coffee.

"You sure do love your coffee," she said, thinking back to the night before.

Trigga nodded and took another sip, licking his soft, wet lips. "Another part of my heritage.

There are a hundred uses for coffee where I'm from."

"You were born in Haiti?"

"No, but I grew up among its people. It's who I am, even if I've never been to the mother island."

She nodded, and glanced at the bulge on his hip. "Since I'm gonna be trusting you, tell me more about who you are."

From his expression, he knew where the conversation would lead. "Anything in particular?"

"What you do for a living."

"What do you think I do?"

"I think you hurt people." He showed a flash of guilt. "Maybe even kill people."

"And what would you know about that?" he asked, a bit defensive, probably about being figured out so easy.

She squared him up. "I might not come across as hood, but I saw some shit growing up, Trigga. My Daddy and uncles were hustlers, and my brother is too. And don't even get me started on my momma..."

"Damn, Ms. Nyka. The look on your face when you said that. What about your momma?"

"You're trying to change the subject," she said, even though she was sure he was right about her reaction to mentioning Sister Treece. "Besides, my issues with my mother are none of your concern."

"You really think that after everything we been through? You concerns are my concerns."

It made Nyka feel something to hear him say that, but she couldn't shake the inescapable fact that, despite what her heart was telling her otherwise, *she didn't know this man*.

"That's sweet, Trigga, but why should I open myself all the way up to you when you won't even be real about the few questions I have about you?"

He gave her a sheepish, disarming grin. "All right, tit for tat," he said, breaking off a piece of pancake and chewing on it. "I work for my cousin in a sometimes...volatile...line of work. Sometimes people get hurt. Or worse. But that's the game, right, and a brotha does what he gotta do. Now, about your momma?"

Nyka fought the impulse to roll her eyes at his zig-zag answer. *Sometimes people get hurt?* She's seen him shoot Derryk between the eyes. She'd witnessed him damn near fight that high-yellow boy of his to the death. All this had happened within a few hours of knowing him!

Seemed like a lot more than just 'sometimes', but then again, judging from the few she'd known in her life, island niggas had a loose definition of time, anyway.

She'd let it go and not press too hard at the point. At least he'd shed some light on who he was working for.

"Alright. Well, my momma and I, we don't see eye-to-eye on very much. I don't like the way she treats people. She damn near broke my daddy, and ended up getting him killed, and I've spent my life not tryin' to be like what I saw from her."

Trigga nodded, not looking her in the eye. "I can understand that," he said in a low tone.

"How so?"

"My Papa wasn't a good man, neither."

"Oh, I see. Do you ever talk to him?"

"No," Trigga said flatly, suddenly tense.

"So you gonna share the same way you made me?" Nyka said, leaning on her elbows. What was good for the goose.

Trigga hesitated and looked Nyka deep into her eyes. For a moment, they looked into each other's, searching for that thing people who trust each other share.

"He used to lay hands on my mama. One night it went too far, and someone died."

Nyka could see the pain on his face, and regretted that she'd help bring back those memories by insisting he answer. "Damn, Trigga, I'm so sorry. You know what? Maybe we should just eat."

With the same quickness he'd used to cut he bindings, Trigga's hands were at her face, cupping her chin firmly, but in a way not meant to hurt her, but to capture her attention.

"No need to apologize, Ms. Nyka. You have every right to know a little more about me. Lord knows, our relationship has been one sided so far."

"Our long, 12 hour relationship," she wryly joked.

"Ha! Yeah," he laughed. "Listen, Nyka, I know I'm not completely open with you just yet, and there are reasons for that you gon' have to trust, but just believe that the reason Derryk's dead right now isn't just because he messed with the wrong people,

it was because of what he was
going to do to you."

"What wrong people?"

"My people from the Gulf
Coast."

Nyka let that sink for a
minute, before asking the question
she'd been wanting to ask all
along.

"Why were you there at the
hotel last night, Trigga?"

"To keep tabs on Derryk, and
to make sure he came through on
his promises."

Nyka studied him, and he
studied her in response. She knew
he wasn't giving her the whole

truth, but had a feeling she
didn't want to know it all anyway.

"You think he was going to
kill me last night?" she asked,
afraid to admit to herself the
answer.

"I've seen that look in a
man's eye before," Trigga replied,
making Nyka wonder about what
happened with his parents.

"So...your mother's dead?"

"No. She ain't the one who's
dead."

They both took an awkward sip
of coffee. Before Nyka could ask
him to clarify what he meant, he'd
impaled a huge portion of pancake

onto a fork and stuffed it into her mouth. They both laughed at the act. Where Nyka was from, a woman feeding a man was something expected, but a man feeding a woman? That was intimacy, right there. And as Trigga went for another piece to place at her lips, Nyka didn't try to stop him.

Was she feeling vulnerable? Damn right. Maybe this was one of those weird hostage situations she'd read about, where people at gunpoint started to catch feels for the people with the guns. Or maybe Nyka was just one of those silly hoes who got as wet from a cocked revolver as they did from a hard dick.

And speaking of dicks, the way Trigga sat on the bed, one leg draped over the edge, one folded in front of him, it made the imprint of his dick all the more apparent. She'd noticed it last night at the club, and it seemed all the more impressive in the light of day.

She felt herself craning her neck, her body involuntarily begging him to feed her more, to give her more. All those feelings, all those emotional twists and turns of the last night, of Derryk and Trigga and blood and bullets...all that shit must've had a warped effect on her, because a rational Nyka could never be acting the way she was right now.

"Open up wide," he said softly, with bass. Her lips wrapped around the food as it entered her mouth, a dribble of syrup dropping to her chin. She chewed, and watched as he wet his thumb, LL Cool J-style, and used it to wipe her clean.

"Can't have you getting dirty on me. At least, not just yet, lil Ma," he said, the look in his eyes as he said it dead serious about its implications. This man wanted her, and he didn't care to wait.

"I feel dirty," she admitted to herself moreso to him. "I feel like I ain't showered in a whole week." She pulled away and rubbed at her arms. She really did feel filthy, but also a bit afraid of where this thing with Trigga was about to lead.

He pointed to a door to the right, his face showing disappointment. "There's a shower through there. There aren't many clean towels, or anything else here, but I managed to scrounge up something for you."

She gave him a smile and walked into the bathroom, her legs weak from no only being tied up, but from the rush of blood from them to her sweet spot above.

Damn, it wasn't right how Trigga made her feel. She closed the door and immediately crouched against it, her hands moving to her pussy. Yeah, she needed a shower all right. A cold as fuck one. She looked around at the dingy bathroom, and wondered where the hell she was. Judging by the spotted wallpaper and the overflowing trashcan, it sure as hell wasn't in a hotel. Going by the toiletries, the place belonged to a woman.

A nasty ass bitch, probably, but a woman nonetheless.

"Whose place is this, Trigga?" she yelled, but Nyka got no response. Any other time, she'd refuse to clean herself up in a strange place, especially one in this condition, but she felt so damn dirty and the spot between her legs ached.

Nyka had always been attracted to a bit of an edge. That's one reason Derryk got to dick her down so early in their relationship. But with Trigga it went beyond physical attraction and sexual longing. Just thinking about what he'd already done for her, what he would do for her, made her feel weak.

No, it wasn't right. Just a day earlier, she'd been whining like a crushed schoolgirl about Derryk pushing her to the side for some other trick with a little bit of cash. And now, she found herself stripping down and letting the cold water of the shower run over her skin as she slowly played with her clit.

Everything that had happened weighed down on her, an accumulation of having her world shattered. She felt angry, sad, scared, and most of all guilty. She'd seen her fiancé die. She'd caught feelings for another man, the same man who killed her fiancé. She'd almost been killed, and was now on the run with a man she barely knew.

And here she was, in a stranger's shower, her hand

between her legs, caressing
herself thinking about the sexy,
dangerous, violent, yet gentle
slice of island chocolate in the
next room.

The warm water flowed across
the goosebumps of her skin. She
bit her lip as she quickened the
pace, her fingers carelessly
slipping in and out of the folds
of her pussy. She found a nice
rhythm, and let herself fantasize
about Trigga, how a man like that
could take anything he wanted from
her. Could do anything he wants.

It was still too soon to
imagine giving herself over to
another man. She'd made a
commitment to Derryk, and even

though he was dead, she took those vows seriously. But there was nothing wrong with imagining being taken, right?

She bit hard as she finally came, and then slid down the shower wall into the tub below, where she finally let herself cry.

CHAPTER FOURTEEN

TRIGGA

Trigga couldn't let himself get too mad about Nyka pulling away. What was it that he was expecting so soon from the woman, anyway? For her to let him run in her just because he told her about his mean ol' Papa? For her to be ready to give up everything for him, some brother she barely knew? The past few hours had been a ride on the crazy train, and poor girl needed time to adjust. To be honest, he was surprised she was doing as well as she did.

Not many women could watch a man get killed right in front of them and be strong enough to have her head on right the next morning. But Nyka wasn't many women. He knew that, and he hoped she did too. Girl was made of some strong stuff. That Haitian-grade stuff, like his mama. Give that girl a knife and a mission, and she'd probably bring the world to its knees.

But he'd have to take it slow with the "we" stuff. Coming on strong would only push her away.

Anyway, he'd already risked everything to keep her alive; he didn't have jack else to prove on that front, at least not right now. Things would work out. It was Fate, right?

What he did need to worry about, though, was keeping them both alive long enough to get to the future he was sure Fate set aside for them. He'd told Crux he'd let him know what was up by that morning, but he had a bad feeling that Veeda got to him first. What Trigga had done was the ultimate violation of the Hitter's Code, and a betrayal of Crux and GCM as a whole. He put a woman, a loose end, a stranger, above his duties to his fam. As long as he continued to protect Nyka, there'd be no coming back from it.

Trigga felt it in his bones that he was a dead man walking, unless he figured out a solution, and fast.

He reached under the bed and took out his bag. He found his phone and placed the battery back into it just long enough to turn it on and read any new messages.

CUZ, GET BCK 2 ME ASAP!!!!

As he suspected, Crux was not a happy man, and an unhappy Crux was a deadly Crux. No choice but to face the fat lady and hit him back, but just as he was about to get ready and make the call, another text made its way to his phone.

THINK ABOUT MY OFFER?

He didn't know what game Veeda was playing, but he'd been her pawn before and had no intention of being one again. She was a living, breathing, walking puppet master, with long legs and wet lips. To his regret, he'd gotten a taste of it once. Running up in her had been the biggest mistake of his life. It was before her marriage to Crux, but it still felt like a betrayal, and had done nothing but rear itself to haunt him ever since.

"Is it from your people on the Gulf Coast?"

Trigga looked up at Nyka, wrapped in a terry cloth towel but still damn from head to toe. Drops of water dripped from the bun she'd tied her hair into. Girl was all natural right now, nothing but soft skin and plump curves, and it took all for him not to jump across the room and pull that towel onto the floor where it belonged.

"Yeah. I need to check in and get this situation right, so we can bounce in peace, that's all."

"Well, can I go home?"

"No!"

He hadn't meant to yell at her like that, but the last thing he needed was for her to do something stupid like go back to her house or contact her people.

"Trigga, enough with the bullshit. Why did your friend try to kill me last night?" she asked, arms crossed, attitude back on high.

"He wasn't my friend," he explained.

"Whatever. Why did he want me dead?"

"It's complicated. I promise you I'll explain it to you when the time's right."

"Nah, nigga, you'll explain now!" she said, picking up a pair of scissors that had been hidden on top of the dresser. "You think you can buy me some pancakes and rub my thighs and I'd go weak-bitch, but I ain't the one. I'm thinking straight now."

Trigga raised his hands in submission. This woman was wild.

He loved it.

Damn straight she deserved to know more than he was telling her, but admitting what type of man he was and what type of nastiness she was now a part? It scared him that she'd run away.

"Okay, Ms. Nyka. Okay. I'll tell you what you want to know. Just put the scissors down."

"How about I put these down, if I feel like it, after you give me the info I want?"

Trigga chuckled. "Alright. But don't say I didn't warn you."

"I'm a big girl," she said, sitting on the edge of the dresser, all the while keeping the blade high and ready. "I think I can handle it.

"Now, why did that nigga Wild try to kill me?"

Trigga hesitated, but knew he was out of options but the truth.

He'd just have to pray for the best.

"Because my Cuz, the person we work for, wants your land and Dante's Inferno free and clear. No strings attached."

"So that's why Derryk's dead too?"

"I told you, the reason Derryk's dead is because he was going to kill you!"

"But were you not going to kill him anyway, muthafucker?" she asked, he eyes wide.

"Yes."

She kept the cold look on her face, but Trigga could tell she was about to break.

"And what about me? Were *you* going to kill me?"

"Naw," he said, half-lying. She was a loose-end, so of course he'd have been the order to murk her. "But...knowing Veeda, I think she made that Derryk's job before I did him in."

With those words, her face dropped. Nyka tried to keep the knife upright, but her arms started shaking. He face covered with tears, and she finally lay on the bed, defeated. He knew she wanted to die at that moment, and he couldn't blame her. No matter what Derryk was and how he had treated her, she was a loyal chick to him, even in his death.

"Everything changed when I met you, though," Trigga said softly, taking the scissors from her tired hands. "Listen, your man Derryk, he got himself in some bad stuff, messing with Veeda and my cuz. I'm sure he still loved you, Ma, but he wasn't left with many choices.

"That man sold his soul."

He helped her up, hoping his words would help her a little bit. How much of what he said was true, even Trigga didn't know. But he couldn't imagine any man willfully throwing a gem like Nyka away for a little bit of fool's gold. Pulling Nyka's sobbing frame into him, he almost felt a bit of sympathy for Derryk, something he never would have before. *Damn girl has already made me a better man.* Besides, Derryk wasn't the first man to get turned every way but right because of Veeda. He probably wouldn't be the last, either.

"I gave everything to him," Nyka whispered softly. "And it wasn't enough."

He lifted her face softly by the chin. "It's not your fault he went bad, Ms. Nyka."

"But I should've been good enough to keep it from happening."

It broke Trigga's heart to hear Nyka's voice crack under those words. Whatever hole had grown in Derryk's heart when it came to Nyka, would never come close to how swelled she'd made Trigga's.

He leaned into her and their lips met. He gave her a kiss-- their first *real* one--and savored the softness. For a couple of seconds, time froze as they both stood there in the moment. Then Nyka slowly tried to buck away, moving her head to the side, leaving Trigga's mouth to brush her cheek.

"No, I...I can't," she said, he voice raspy and tired. "This isn't right."

Trigga slipped his hand around her backside and up her towel. He gave her thick buttocks a firm squeeze. She responded by biting her lips, a small moan escaping her throat. He could tell from her face he'd just hit her where she wasn't expecting, somewhere sensitive. She was at the edge, he could feel it. He pulled her closer so she could feel how close he was too.

"Your body says somethin' else," he whispered in her ear. She practically shivered with his words. She gently pushed against his chest, but it was a weak gesture. He responded by grabbing both buttocks with his hands and lifting her onto the dresser.

Trigga gently trailed his lips from his ears to her cheeks and then her lips. She met his lips with her own. Soft, thick, wet lips that made Trigga's dick jump. So sweet.

And he bet if he slipped his fingers between her thighs, he'd find those other lips ready too. He slowly began to undo her towel.

"No!" Nyka said firmly, though pants and huffs. "I...I just can't Trigga. Please!" She pushed him away.

Trigga stood confused, the front of his pants close to ripping, her eyes helplessly locked in on it.

This woman had him going every which way. If it had been anyone else, he'd be angry enough to shoot someone, but with Nyka, he tried his best to keep control. "What's wrong?" he finally said.

She closed her eyes in an attempt to compose herself. "I'm not that kind of woman, Trigga."

"What do you mean?" He cupped her chin towards him and waited for her to finally look at him. "You sending me mixed signals here, Ms. Nyka."

"I don't mean to, but you have to understand!" Her eyes were close to swelling with tears again. "Just a day ago my heart belonged to another man. I know he did me wrong. I know he tried to kill me! But I can't just turn my heart off like that. I won't be like her!"

Trigga furrowed his brow, disappointed but not as broken as he'd have expected. "Like who?"

"Like my mother. I won't be the type of woman who spreads her legs on a whim, to any man who shows her attention or a few dollars."

Trigga backed away. Issues with a parent? That's something he understood. Trying your best not to be that person every day? Oh yeah. He knew exactly where Nyka was coming from. He let the excitement fade, his heartbeat to settle, and his erection to subside.

He'd gotten caught up in the moment and tried to do the exact thing he said he wouldn't do. Push her. He was still a stranger to her, and he needed to remember that. Plus, he'd have to earn her trust the old fashioned way.

In her mind, there was still a lot of mystery surrounding the past 12 hours, and it would take a while to clear everything up. He could tell from the way she let him caress her cheek that she knew he wouldn't hurt her, but Trigga had no doubt that she still saw him as a dangerous man. A killer.

"It's okay, Ms. Nyka. We got caught up there for a second." He turned and tidied himself. He grabbed his bag and took out an old cell. "Take this. There's only one number programmed into it, and it's to the phone I'll be using. I'm trusting you not to use it for anything else. Until I get this bounty off your head, you can't drag anyone into this. Not the police, not your fam, not your friends. Straight?"

She nodded.

"Good."

"Where are you going?" she asked, following him as he left the bedroom and entered a narrow hallway leading to a messy living room.

"I'm gonna try to get a handle of where we stand. There some more stuff going on than just us moving in on your club."

As he was about to exit the front door, Nyka noticed the unconscious woman lying face down on a couch, her booty shorts still riding up from the night prior at the club.

"Is that muthafucking KD!!??"

Trigga laughed. "Shorty gave me her number and address last night, and this was the only place I could think of to go. Don't worry, your girl will be fine, just knocked out for a few hours."

"Should've killed this bitch, too," he heard Nyka mumble as he stopped out the door.

Trigga smirked. This girl was something else. He took out the set of keys he'd found in KD's kitchen and unlocked her hoopty. It smelled of old perfume and tuna, but it would have to do. He had no idea who would be out looking for the vehicle he'd driven the night before. Better safe than sorry.

He turned on his phone and scrolled through the messages. He honed in on the last one sent by Veeda and hit reply.

After he'd sent his response, he fired up the whip and took off. He needed to think. Bad enough Nyka had his mind and emotions turned every which way. Emotions couldn't be controlled, though. What really got him was the thought of his sloppiness putting her in danger. Although Trigga was a hitter, he knew he wouldn't be one for life. There should've been an escape plan. There should've been an out that no one--not Crux, not Veeda, not anyone GCM--knew about.

He should've had a special place set up someone remote, nice and paid for. He should've had a backup vehicle in storage in a fake name. He should've had passports and fake IDs on the ready just in case he had to make a quick escape.

But no. He'd gotten comfortable, and almost all his funds were tied to GCM. He was completely trackable, meaning his options were limited. Trigga had no intention of ever turning his back on his cuz, but he should've seen this day coming when he'd have to make a choice to step away. If Nyka was who he thought she was--his destiny--Trigga knew his days as a right hand to Crux were numbered.

He deserved happiness, but the motto "GCM for life" meant something. Not to mention that the woman he wanted stood in the way of Crux and his money. He'd been tasked to oversee her death, if she got in the way. On top of that, Veeda needed her dead too. But not only was she not dead, the entire operation all around had gone haywire.

Crux wanted Dante's. He wanted Nyka's land. He wanted to expand his territory and his influence in the worst way. Nyka was now in the way.

Crux must've sent Veeda to oversee a part of the operation while Trigga took care of the rest. *Never let anyone see too much of the big picture, not even your right hand hitter.* From what Trigga could figure, Nyka was supposed to die first, after signing away her land to Derryk, then Trigga would've murked Derryk, leaving everything to his new GCM partners. No loose ends.

What would happen now, Trigga had no idea. Except for the fact that he'd kill anyone who tried to hurt Nyka, even if it meant that person was his fam.

The phone beeped. Trigga read
the text, and set off in response.

CHAPTER FIFTEEN

WILD

"Ow. Goddamnit, OW!!!" Wild yelled through clenched teeth as his half-Choctaw shorty sewed the hole in his leg.

"Stop being such a little pussy, baby."

"Fuck that shit hurts. Aren't you squaws supposed to be magic with medicine and shit, anyway?"

Red rolled her eyes and continued her work. Wild knew she hated we he started with the racist 'squaw' stuff, but hell if he cared at that moment. The makeshift bandage job Red had done the night before had come undone while they were fucking, and now he was letting her stitch him up right. Supposedly her uncle had been a medicine man or some shit, and a part-time paramedic, and had taught her a few things about emergency care.

But damn if he could tell that right now.

At that moment it seemed like she was just poking at him for the hell of it, and goddamn if he didn't already hate needles.

"I'm not a fucking doctor, *nigga*," she said, sassing at him in a way that made her titties shake in her tank top. "And if you want it done right, you should go to the hospital like a normal person would."

Wild grabbed her by her long, black hair, and pulled her face towards his. "Just because your daddy Big Red had you with his black girlfriend doesn't mean you get to call a nigga *nigga* anytime you want. Feel me?"

She jerked her head away and stuck her tongue out. "Whatever...nigga," she said, getting back to work.

"Your mouth gonna get you in trouble, little girl." Wild eyed Red, getting hard just thinking about what was under her tank top and booty shorts. Wild had had his share of women. Where he was from, they flocked to him like gnats. He was a young nigga with good looks and a big future. A young hitter with the GCM on his way up. Pussy had never been a thing for him.

But he couldn't lie. Red was different. He definitely felt her in a way those other Gulf Coast bitches couldn't match. Like him, she hadn't been raised in the most stable home. They were both bastards who'd been thrown away by a parent and had to find their way in a world that didn't want them. And like Wild, Red refused to give up without a hell of a fight.

Messing with a chick on the job wasn't ideal, and lord knows what Veeda would do when she found out his true feelings for Red. But the heart feels what it feels.

Besides, Red was sexy as fuck, petite with brown skin and Indian features. And she had a pouty mouth that made his man stand up just looking at it.

Oh yeah, he was feeling her. But the job came first, and no matter how guilty he felt, he wouldn't forget why he'd gotten with her in the first place.

"Wild, be serious for a minute. Why won't you tell me what happened to you?"

He sighed in frustration. "I told you, you don't need to know all that."

She stood her and put her hands on her hip. "You come in here bleeding all over my apartment, and you don't think I need to know what's going on? Don't think I didn't hear there was a shooting at the hotel last night?"

"Well, if you think you know every goddamn thing, why the fuck did you ask?"

"Because I need to hear it from you! I'm not some dumb bitch, Wild. I know you do some dangerous things for a living. But you continuously lying to me makes me think you don't care about me at all."

"Don't even start that shit," Wild said, gingerly standing up to tower over her. He lifted her chin and gave her a kiss. "I can't tell you everything that's going on just yet. Just believe that I'm the good guy in all this. You know I'm crazy about you."

She gave him wet eyes. "For real?"

"For real." He sat back down on her kitchen chair. "Now finish this shit. Damn!"

"You such an asshole," she said, getting back on her knees and tending his wound.

Wild closed his eyes to block out the pain. Thankfully she'd only heard a few random things about what went down at the hotel. Damn right he felt guilty for treating his girl that way, but that's the way it had to be.

He'd officially met Red a month ago at Dante's, but she'd been in his and Trigga's scope even longer. A paralegal, she handled all of the paperwork concerning Dante's and the land surrounding it from the very beginning.

And not only that, she was one of Nyka's girls, and had been giving him information about her, Derryk, and Dante's from the very beginning. Some bitches just liked to talk a lot when they were getting good dick.

"OW!!! What the fuck, Squaw?"

"Call me that one more time and I'm going to stick this needle in your dick!' she cheesed. "Just calm down. I'm almost done. You sure you don't want something for your pain?"

"Unless it's weed, hell no. I ain't touching any of your peyote shit." His momma had been an addict even before he was born, and he'd seen what it did to her. That shit made her the type of woman to give up on her son and sell out her own daughter for the next hit.

Naw, he'd never touch that shit, no matter how good it would make him feel right now.

If it wasn't for Veeda, there's no telling where he'd be. That's why failing her was not an option. He glanced at his phone and saw new messages waiting for him, all from her. This situation

with Trigga and Nyka needed to be
rectified, and fast.

"You sure you ain't heard from
your girl?"

Red looked at him, hesitating
before speaking. "No, and why are
you still so interested in her?"

"I told you, I was hired by
her business partners to make sure
this Gulf Coast deal goes down
without a hitch. Background shit
and behind the scenes shit. I'm
just trying to make sure she's
alright." It didn't matter how
ridiculous the lie sounded, he
knew Red would go along with it
for the simple fact that she was
falling for him.

"No, she was supposed to holla back at me last night. Baby, she's not in danger, is she?"

He looked her in her eyes. "Naw, I'd never let that happen. I told you, I'm looking out for her. The last thing my people want is for something bad to happen to your girl before the money changes hands."

She gave him a long glance and then finished stitching his leg. After bandaging it, she sat on the table, by his side. "Better now?"

"It will be once you give me some of that pussy," Wild said, rubbing her leg.

"Such a dirty muthafucker," she said and gave him a soft kiss. "I forgot to mention, I finished the paperwork you asked for."

"Where is it?"

"In my purse. Wild, you sure I'm not getting Nyka in trouble by doing all this for you? I already feel guilty running my mouth to you about her business and not telling her."

"Damn, I told you I'm looking out for her!"

"I know, but..."

"But nothing. Squaw, you helping her out, and you're helping me help her."

"That's what you tell me," she mumbled. He gave her a kiss on her neck. "And nigga, if you call me Squaw one more time..."

"What are you going to do?"

"Imma scalp your yellow ass, that's what," she said playfully.

"You ain't gonna do shit except what I tell you."

"And who the fuck do you think you're talking t..."

Before she could finish, Wild flipped her hard on the table, her torso and face down, her legs hanging over the table's end.

"Wild! What are you doi..."

Red slapped her ass hard, just the way she liked it. He then rubbed her ass, letting her know it was on. She squeezed her legs together in delight.

"You got a smart ass mouth, Squaw. I'm tired of having to set you straight!" he said, slipping her booty shorts below her knees. The spot where he'd smacked her was already red. He kissed it, eliciting a visible shiver.

"That's 'cause you say stupid shit to me, Wild," she tried to say, but he voice was weak. "I don't know why you think I'm going to give you some while you keep lying to me."

"Ain't nobody lying to you, girl, and you're going to give it to me because this pussy belongs to me, doesn't it?"

"NOOooooo!" she moaned in delight as Wild lifted her until she was kneeling completely on the table. He rapidly got to work, slipping his tongue between her folds, savoring the immediate wetness.

He slowly moved over her pussy, methodically, up and down. After every few strokes, he let the tip of his tongue slip inside, fucking her wetness with his tongue. After her moaning became continuous, he started on her clit, softly sucking on it until Red started to buckle.

"Oh, Wildddd!" she purred, close to cumming. Of all the women Wild had been with, Red was the first with whom he was so in tune with sexually. Most bitches would just get the dick and a shot of his seed, but with Red it was different. He wanted to please her. He wanted to make her want him more than anything else in the world.

She came in his mouth, filling it with juice. Wild flipped her on her back and unzipped his pants.

"No baby. I just fixed you wound."

Instead of answering, Wild slipped his dick into her waiting pussy. One stroke, two stroke three...it didn't take long before she buckled under his grip. Girl acted crazy as hell when she was getting it, as crazy as he could be in most situations.

He loved the way he made her feel. It was a new situation, giving someone else pleasure like that. Wild considered himself damaged and hard, incapable of truly making someone else happy. It's why he knew he'd chosen to be a hitter. It's the only way he knew to survive. To get others before they could get him first.

But with Red, he knew things could be different. Veeda taught him that no other woman would ever be as good to him as she could be, but now he knew she was wrong.

"I'm cummmminnnnggg!" Red screamed, digging her nails into his shoulders. He let her finish and then pushed her to the floor. He pushed himself in hard and stroked until he finally came.

"Goddamn, Squaw. My pussy feeling right!" he said as they lay on the floor.

She rubbed his face and touched his lips. "You're so full of shit, Wild. You can't even tell me the truth about what you do, and you still think I belong to you."

"Because you do."

"Until you leave me," she said, getting up and heading to the bathroom. Wild blew out a frustrated breath and tried to keep his cool. He understood where her insecurities came from.

From her father. Sure, he was around, *but he wasn't really there*, you know? That part-time father, sometimes acknowledgment shit had taken a toll on his girl.

And Wild knew from experience that that fear of abandonment never went away. What made it all the worse was yeah, she was right that maybe he would have to leave pretty soon.

But Wild had a plan. He didn't intend to give Red up without a fight, no matter what his Aunt Vee had to say about the matter. But unlike that traitor Trigga, Wild had the smarts to have his cake and eat it too.

Turning on GCM could never happen. It *would* never happen, but that didn't mean he couldn't fit red into the equation.

As he got up to zip his pants, Red's phone began to vibrate. He reached for it, but she quickly reappeared and snatched it away.

"Oh, it's like that, huh?" he said as she checked her messages. The more she read, the more worried she looked.

"Who is it, Squaw?"

She didn't respond.

"I said, who the fuck is it?!" he said, running up on her. She defensively held the phone to her chest, irritating him all the more.

"Not everything is your business, Wild!"

The fuck it wasn't. After just fucking the hell out of her, Wild wasn't about to suddenly let this chick make a fool of him. If it was another nigga, he'd kill her.

He snatched the phone from her hands, fending her off as she fought. Scrolling through the messages, he bit his lip with satisfaction.

"You were gonna keep this shit from me?" he said angrily, and he got ready to leave.

"You keep all kinds of shit from me! And what do you want with Nyka now?"

He put on his shoes and got his keys. "I just gotta finish some business. I promise, I'm coming back for you. You just need to trust me, Squaw."

He left her cursing behind, taking out his phone to text his aunt. Things were about to go down. He now knew where Nyka was hiding.

CHAPTER SIXTEEN

TRIGGA

It took a while for Trigga to finally make it to the address given to him, but once he did, he instantly knew it was a Veeda type of joint. The house sprawled over at least an acre of country that was freshly manicured and immaculately cared for.

He wondered who the house belonged to and what Veeda had had to do to use it. Probably some rich old hustler with a sagging manhood that only responded to Veeda's gentle command. Give it to the girl, she knew how to coax a man and get the desired result. Brothers stayed happy to be stupid for her.

He sat in the car for a few more minutes, listening to Jay-Z's *Forever Young*. None of this felt right. He didn't trust Veeda, and he knew there was a lot more going on than just a play for Nyka's club and the land attached to it.

Haitian intuition had taken Trigga far in life, and right now that intuition screamed to him to turn around and go back to Nyka.

He'd been so close to breaking down her walls, and he was more than ready to try again. Giving her space, and letting her get over her hurdles, well, that sounded like the right thing to do, but being around her made him want to speed up the process whether she thought she was ready or not.

Nyka had his world twisted, his mind messed up. So much so, he'd entertained Veeda's suggestion to have this meeting and break bread. Pure desperation, but what else could he do? At some point, Crux would get tired of sitting around waiting for his cousin to see the light. And with Veeda whispering in his ear, turning cousin against cousin, Trigga lived on borrowed time.

After a few more minutes of contemplation, Trigga finally got out of the car. Making his way up the walkway, he cautiously looked left and right for any signs of trouble, his hand never an inch from his piece.

"You really think I'd ambush you, Trigga?" Veeda's silky voice said from the now open door. Trigga stopped and glanced. Draped, barely, in a silk robe that exposed her soft bosom, her fingers brushed her glistening thighs. "I'd never do that to you. Didn't you read your tea leaves before coming here?"

"Not even the eyes of fate can get a handle of you, Veeda," he said, stepping past her into a vast foyer. Despite Nyka weighing so much on his mind, Trigga wouldn't be a man if he didn't take notice the sweet smell of baby oil coming from Veeda's body. Even devils can be sexy in lingerie.

"I'm not that hard to read, Trigga. In fact," she said, sashaying and leading him into a sitting area, "you were pretty damn good at reading me many nights long ago."

Trigga pursed his lips. "That was before you and Crux were a thing."

"Whatever that thing is." She picked up a glass and took a sip of drink. "Can I pour you something?"

"No thank you."

"It's not poison, see?" she said, dipping a finger in her glass and bringing it to Trigga's lips. "Take a lick."

Angrily, Trigga grabbed her wrist. "I didn't come here for this. I need you to fix this thing

with Nyka, and I need you to do it
now!"

She laughed and snatched away
her arm. "Damn, Trigga. She got
you whipped already? Your Haitian
cousins would be ashamed."

"My Haitian cousins appreciate
good women. When they can find
one, anyway." He wound to wound
Veeda with the insult. "Nobody's
going to hurt Nyka. You can get
what you want without killing
anyone. We don't have to play it
this way."

She smiled a cat-like smile.
"I think we're going to play it
any way I damn well see fit. And
just so *you* understand: we don't

have to do business here, Trigga.
You can just turn around and drive
back to your country bitch and
live happily ever after."

Trigga let out a frustrated
sigh.

"Oh, that's right. You can't.
Sooner or late one of Crux's
bullets would mess up her grit-
and-cheese face. So, your choice.
Play or don't play."

Trigga said nothing. He didn't
have a choice but to play for now.
He was committed to getting Nyka
off Crux's hit list and,
hopefully, convincing her they
were meant to be together.

"Good. Now take off your gloves, Trigga dear. You make a sista think you want to kill her or something." The idea had crossed Trigga's mind, to come in here, put an end to Veeda in his life for good, and pray to God he could break bread with Crux. Cuz could easily find another chick to be his official woman. It's not like he didn't have many in waiting, anyway. Not that Trigga approved, but he understood a man like Crux had a big appetite that not even a bad chick like Veeda could fill.

Trigga slipped off his gloves and waited for Veeda to tell him what to do next. "Okay. You win.

What do you want from me? And what are you really up to? I know you, Veeda, and this is about more than just a club."

"No shit, nigga," she said, surprising him with her bluntness. "And I'll more than happily explain it to you when I feel like it. You're here only because I want you here. Don't forget who's in control." She brought him a glass of bubbly liquid. "Now drink and sit down."

He took the glass and sniffed it, eying Veeda as she licked her finger. He took a sip of the sweet, yet bitter liquid, before finally gulping down the rest, to Veeda's delight.

"Now, was that so hard, baby?
Now sit."

Trigga did as he was told,
paying attention to Veeda's every
move. She sat down cross-legged on
the sofa across from him, the
fabric of her robe bare covering
the top of her shaved womanhood.
She smiled, noticing what he was
eying.

"So you have me here, Veeda.
Now what?"

"Now we wait."

"For what?"

"For the drugs to set in."

The moment she said it, he
felt the effects. It wasn't that

he was groggy, but everything about him seemed heavy. He attempted to move his arms, and all they did was brush the expensive fabric of the couch below him. Even the outlines of his vision seemed heavier, as if everything had more depth. Veeda let out a cackling laugh.

"Nigga, what did you expect?" She got up and walked towards him. "Muthafuckers and the pussy they lose their minds over. First Wild and his dumb ass gets sprung on some half-Indian bitch, and even you. The big, bad Trigga. Brought down by some country pussy he could buy half-priced back home."

Trigga tried to move his mouth, to talk, but his tongue weighed a ton. The words came out in slow motion. "What...are...you..."

Veeda stood behind him now, playing in his scalp with her nails. "What am I doing? I'm taking what's mine, baby."

She kissed his ear, slowly easing her tongue inside the lobe. "That used to turn you on? Does it still?" She sucked on it more, slowly moving her hand down his chest to his pants and onto his manhood.

"I see the answer is yes."

Trigga tried to regain control, but he couldn't fight the fact Veeda still knew his spots. He sat immobilized as she continued to play with his ear and then moved down to his neck.

"You were always good dick, Trigga, but don't get it twisted," she whispered in his ear. "I could have any man I want. The only reason I'm messing with you is because I like to fuck with my prey before I kill."

She moved back to Trigga's front and unbuttoned his shirt. She took his gun and kissed the barrel, before unloading and throwing it to the side. Trigga let out a heavy sigh of relief that she wouldn't put a bullet in his brain.

He felt relieved, but knew he might be in store for much, much worse.

Veeda began to kiss his chest, her lips as wet and soft as he remembered. As she did so, Trigga's mind began to wander back to the times he and Veeda had been a thing. Back then, he only knew her as one of Crux's women. Nothing special. His cuz had practically a harem back then, and Veeda--as fine as she was--didn't merit a second thought.

That was, until Trigga got to know her. Ol' girl was driven and smart, far from the other hot-air tricks that gravitated towards young Haitian hustlers on the Coast. There was a vulnerability about here that Trigga could relate to.

Damaged goods, the both of them. Born hustlers ready to scrap. It didn't long before he was running up in her, her sophistication a turn on for his sexual need. She wore pearl necklaces when she gave him head. She draped herself in Gucci and Prada as she rode him like a woman in heat. She showed herself to be the cunning, tough chick a hard-core Haitian would love to tame.

All qualities any man in Trigga's position would admire, which was exactly why Crux elevated her in the GCM and then into his bedroom.

After that, the thing between him and Veeda? Straight over. No matter how much she wanted to creep.

And as her lips slowly made their way down his chest, with jazz playing in the background, with drugs making him weak, he couldn't help but remember the times.

She unzipped his pants, his man pushing against his drawers in spite of his wishes. She looked up

at him with hungry eyes, and
smiled.

"Wanna know the first time I
had Haitian dick, Trigga?" she
said, slipping the fabric from
over the head. "Oh, it wasn't you,
or Crux. It was Sinclair Trinidad.
Remember him?"

She lightly licked the tip of
his manhood. Trigga struggled as
he remembered old man Trinidad,
one of the OG refugees who had
come to America with his and
Crux's fathers. Scarface Sinclair
is what they called him, who'd
been sliced up by a machete when
he was a boy, and killed the man
responsible with the same machete

many years later. Or that's how the story goes.

"It was when I was sixteen, and Crux had just found me on a corner. Your cousin wined me, dined me, filled my head with all the things he could do for me. And just when I let my guard down and was beginning to fall for him, you know what he did?

"Sent me to Sinclair for the night to close a deal. You know how Sinclair likes knives, don't you? I still got a couple of marks on my thighs from that night..."

She laughed lightly, scraping her fingernails over his shaft. For the first time since Trigga could remember, he felt fear for himself. Genuine, terrifying fear.

"From that moment on, I knew no nigga would ever save me, could ever save me. Especially not an island one. You almost fooled me into believing otherwise, but even you turned your back on me."

Trigga wanted to say something, but his mouth felt dry and empty. His tongue stayed stuck on pause.

"Don't get me wrong, being with Crux has given me the finest things in life, and I'll always appreciate that," she said, slowly rubbing him up and down. "But as long as I'm with him, I'll be nothing more than a high-class whore. Did you know he sent me down here to fuck that nigga Derryk? To butter him up, and get GCM his club?"

She looked in Trigga's face, and he could tell she was reading him.

"Sure, I'd have volunteered anyway, to secure my paper. But it's the fact that Horatio asked me to do it. The woman who carries his name! What kind of man does that to his wife?"

Trigga wanted to shake his head, to look sympathetic, even though he most assuredly was not. Nobody made Veeda do anything.

Crux only took advantage of what she was happy to do anyway.

"But give it to poor, dead, stupid Derryk. He made me realize something. That I could be more. That I could do more. That's what all of this is about, Trigga. Not just about securing Dante's, but securing my future."

He heard the words but could hardly understand. The room was becoming a black tunnel, and at the end was a face he couldn't recognize. A hallucination.

"I'm going to finalize this deal, all right. But not for Crux. I'm doing it for me. Everything I've done is to make sure that club, that land, belongs to me. All you did was make it easier. I hadn't planned for you to go crazy like you did, to turn against your family, but damn if I'm not going to use this to my advantage."

Veeda's words echoed in his head, but all he could concentrate on was the face. That face at the end of the black tunnel. A face just like the mask he slept with every night, to keep the demons away, to ward off his shame.

"You've given me the perfect opportunity to do what I've wanted to do since that day Crux told me I would marry him, that my body, my pussy was his to do with whatever he pleased, as long as it made him money.

"I'm going to use this opportunity to kill Crux once and for all, and take over all of GCM. How do you like that, Trigga?"

Her words registered. They shook him. But it was the vision he was having that shocked him more. The hallucination got closer and closer, the mask, the face clearer and clearer. It was the face of his Papa. The same face he had right before Trigga shot him dead.

By now, his manhood was in Veeda's mouth, and the pleasure and fear he felt was driving him mad. Around his Papa's face, the scene shifted to that night, as his Papa beat his Mama over and over. In Trigga's hand, he felt the gun he'd used that night. He felt it, heavy and ready to fire its load.

Veeda's strokes sped up, faster and faster. She played with the head with her tongue, using her thumb and finger to stroke at the same time. Trigga felt himself get closer and closer to coming, to pulling the trigger and changing his life forever, making him the man always ready to pull the trigger if the Fates allowed.

"You shouldn't have come here, Trigga," Veeda continued, her

breathing heavy from her other
hand working between her thighs.
"Did you really think I would let
you and that country bitch go? If
I can't have you, no one can."

Trigga's Papa hit his Mama
again. And again. Trigga hands
shook from being so little, from
being so weak, from holding up
such a heavy gun. He was so close
to firing. He was so close to
losing control, to spilling his
seed onto Veeda's vindictive hand.

"Mmmm," Veeda moaned, cumming
from the scene being acted out.
Giving herself a second, she
started stroking Trigga again,
this time with two hands. "Your
dumb little girlfriend gave

herself away. We know where she
is. We have the address. And
Wild's about to finish her once
and for all."

Trigga felt himself snap back,
just before he was about to
explode, just before he was going
to pull the trigger and kill his
Papa in his mind. Nyka.

Nyka.

With all the energy he could
muster, he launched his leg,
sending Veeda flying back against
a glass table. He stood up, barely
able to balance himself, and she
reoriented himself and wiped blood
from her lip.

"Haha. Oh Trigga, baby, did you think I was letting you out of here alive? If Crux dies, you're the next in line. I can't have that," she said, putting out a knife she'd hidden. "A little gift from old Trinidad. I used it to cut off his balls the last time I saw him."

She lunged at Trigga, sending the blade into his ribs. He screamed in pain, Veeda's laughter echoing in his ears.

"No. Nyka..." he mumbled to himself while he struggled to remain conscious. With one last effort, he punched Veeda hard in the face, knocking her out.

Gotta get back. Gotta save her, he thought to himself, making it out of the house and into his car. With shaky, fumbling hands, he tried to call the number of the phone he'd left her. No response.

He banged his head against the steering wheel before finally mustering enough energy to turn the ignition. He wouldn't stay conscious long with the wound to his side, but he had to try to make it back to Nyka.

He had to save the woman of his dreams.

CHAPTER SEVENTEEN

NYKA

Nyka rummaged through drawer after drawer, cabinet after cabinet, with no luck.

"Bitch, you got to have an extra phone around here somewhere!" she screamed at KD, who now sat up on her couch, her hands still bound and mouth covered with tape. Nyka walked to her. "If I uncover your mouth, will you please tell me what I need to know?" KD nodded slowly. Nyka ripped off the tape.

"Bitch, fuck you! When I get out of these ropes, I'm going to kill you! You hear me, you crazy, stuck up bitch! I'm going to..." Nyka quickly stuck the tape back over KD's mouth and rolled her eyes.

"Dumb thot. I was trying to do you a favor." Nyka continued her search through the nasty apartment, being careful to avoid the rat droppings and dead roaches. Ugh.

Nyka took out the phone Trigga had left her and tried the text feature again. Disabled. Trigga definitely didn't want her contacting anyone on the outside. In fact, the only thing she could do was dial the number Trigga had left her for his cell phone. And the longer she sat there in her thoughts, the less she wanted to do even that.

Almost sleeping with the man who had killed her fiancé? Pure craziness, right? Yes, there was something about Trigga that made her trust him against her better judgment, but there was no mistaking the fact that Trigga was an assassin who'd originally been hired to kill her too, if the need demanded.

And now he was risking his life to save her? Something didn't feel right about that. Or at least, that's what she tried her damndest to convince herself. Having feels for Trigga felt like the ultimate betrayal to Derryk, even though Derryk had betrayed her first in the worst ways possible.

Ever since childhood, ever since she'd witnessed how her mother had treated her Daddy, ever since she'd debased herself lying for her mother, covering for her, Nyka had promised herself to be a one-man woman. Nobody understood what it was like, being the daughter of Sister Treece, the wildest woman in Moriah, Mississippi, the woman even pastors wouldn't resist taking to bed.

She'd been expected to be just like her. She already looked like Sister Treece in the face and in the hips. No matter what she did, no matter how far she made it, how well she talked and how properly she dressed, she'd always been Baby Treece, hoe in waiting.

That stuff messed her up in the psyche, made her take vows most modern chick would think retarded. Even giving up it to Derryk and losing her virginity took a miracle, an act of love at first sight. Derryk was supposed to be her forever. Too bad he didn't feel the same.

Still, despite all that, despite his creeping and despite him even trying to kill her, there was a burden of loyalty she couldn't shake. No matter how hot Trigga made her, she wouldn't become the type of woman to slip into a man's bed after a few soft words.

Even though just the thought of him got her warm between her thighs.

No, she had to get out of there before he came back. Leaving

KD's apartment without a place to go was out of the question. She absolutely believed Trigga when he said her life was in danger. She'd seen it herself. But she had people she could trust. If only she could find a phone.

If only she could get in touch with her girl Red.

She moved to KD's bedroom to search from top to bottom. She flipped the mattress of the bed and there it was. A phone. She powered it up and saw it had enough juice to last maybe a few seconds. Not enough to make a call, but maybe enough to send out a quick text.

She typed in Red's number and sent an urgent message, along with the address of KD's place. She then watched the phone go dead, and her heart sank.

She hoped her message got through.

Just thinking about it made her sick to her stomach. Her stomach lurched and Nyka ran to the bathroom, where she threw up for the fourth time in a week.

"Oh please, God, please, don't let this happen now," she said to herself as she wiped her face. Nyka didn't get sick often, and the fact that it was happening so

often lately meant something was
seriously wrong.

And she suspected she knew
what.

She splashed her face with
some water and stared at herself.
Then she rubbed her belly.

No, this couldn't be happening
right now. Right?

She had an idea. A low-end,
thirsty thot like KD must have
what she needed to find out for
sure. Nyka rummaged under KD's
dingy sink until she found the
box, pink and ready to use.

Nyka closed her eyes and
prayed. She let herself get lost

in it, not moving for what felt like forever.

Time passed. First a few minutes, and then much more. Nyka wasn't really that religious, but it took all her effort to rise from her knees.

God, please. She finally finished, and just as she was about to open her eyes, she heard a loud bang in the living room.

KD screamed through her tape. Nyka found the scissors she'd had before on the dresser drawer. She hid it in the waist of her pants and slowly made her way back to the living room.

Standing, with his gun pointed to KD's head, was the crazy yellow nigga she'd met before. Wild. The man she'd shot, and who was back to finish the job.

"Well, look at this shit, y'all. Didn't think you'd see me again so soon, did you?" he said, holding KD tightly against him, like a hostage. KD's eyes swelled with fear. Nyka almost felt sorry that she'd been dragged into her drama.

"Don't even think about moving. Where's my boy, Trigga? I got somethin' for him too," Wild asked, looking at his surroundings. "Answer me!"

Nyka tried to speak, but couldn't. The lump in her throat wouldn't let her. She didn't know what to say anyway.

"I'mma ask you again. Either tell me where Trigga is, or I shoot this bitch right here, right now," he said, tightening his grip on KD and eliciting another scream from her. Nyka and KD met eyes for a second, and they both knew what would happen next.

Sorry, KD.

With all the energy she could muster, Nyka ran, slamming the bedroom door behind.

"God damn!" she heard Wild scream. Nyka desperately tried to find a place to hide. If she ran into the bathroom, there'd be nowhere else to go. She'd be trapped. Hiding under the bed was not an option. Nor was breaking and jumping out the window before Wild could force his way in.

No, it was time to fight. She stood by the door's frame, waiting for Wild to break it down, her scissors raised high.

Wild finally pushed his way through, and Nyka came down hard on his shoulder. He screamed and dropped the gun. Seizing the opportunity, Nyka kicked him hard in his groin, sending him to the ground.

She ran into the living room, where KD writhed on the carpet.

"Aw, fuck," Nyka said to herself and she tried to quickly untie the hoe. From Trigga, Nyka knew enough about Wild to know he was unpredictable. He hadn't killed KD yet, but Nyka wouldn't leave her there defenseless in case the cray nigga decided to change his mind.

"Come on, get up!" she said, helping KD to her feet. "We have to go now!"

There was a loud roar in the air, and both women instinctively raised their hands in defense. Wild stood, his gun pointed in the

air, a pained, crazy look in his
eyes. His free shoulder bleed, its
arm limp.

"Bitch, you gonna pay for
that. If I didn't need you to sign
over your shit, you'd be dead
already. So here's what we're
going to do. You're going to
slowly walk through that door and
into my car. You're going to sign
the paperwork you need to sign to
make my aunt her money, and then
I'm going to slowly watch you die
while I laugh my ass off."

"Muthafucker, I'm not going
anywhere with you!" Nyka said. She
and KD clutched each other, and
for the first time, she felt like
KD was more than just a worthless

hoe. Too bad that realization came too late.

"Wild? Wild, what's going on?" a familiar voice said from behind.

Nyka turned around to see Red, a look of shock on her face.

"Red, go!" Nyka yelled at her friend, who stared shocked at Wild.

"The fuck are you doing here, Squaw?" Wild asked, clearly irritated at Red's sudden presence. "I told you I would handle this."

"Handle this? What is he talking about, Red?" Nyka asked,

confused as all hell and
incredulous.

"I'm so sorry, Nyk. I...I let
him read your text. He told me was
here to help you!" she said,
moving to her friend's side.

"Squaw, get the fuck out of
here before something bad happens.
This has nothing to do with you. I
promise I'll explain this shit
later." Wild's voice sounded
softer, almost pleading. Nyka
could tell that the two were more
than mere acquaintances.

"I'm not going anyway, Wild!
You're not going to hurt my
friend, unless you feel like
hurting me too." She stepped

between Nyka, KD, and Wild.
"Whatever you think you're doing,
you don't have to, Baby. This
isn't you. You're better than
this."

Wild wiped the sweat from his
face. The crazy, unpredictable
negro that had tried to kill Nyka
was suddenly gone, replaced by a
nervous, conflicted child. "You
got no idea what's going on, Red.
My aunt gave me an order, and I
have to follow it. I'm doing this
to make my life better. I'm going
to make all our lives better."

"Stop listening to your aunt,"
she said, slowly stepping closer
to Wild. "She does nothing but use
you. You told me that yourself.

You don't have to be her whipping boy anymore."

Wild bit his lip. Nyka used the moment to squeeze KD's wrist, signaling to her to get ready to run.

"Squaw, you just gotta trust me here," wild said as he attempted to move Red to the side. She didn't budge.

"No."

His hands shook as his gun slowly lowered.

"Put...put the gun down, Wild!" a voice said from the door. It was Trigga, bloodied and pale,

"Trigga!" Nyka cried, he heart feeling heavy.

The craziness in Wild's face returned. He raised his gun. "Oh, I been waiting for this, nigga!"

"Your mistake, young buck," Trigga said, firing his gun.

"No!" Red screamed, realizing what would happen. She jumped in front of Wild before the trigger was pulled.

Red fell to the floor with a bang, moaning in pain. Wild fell to her side. "Damn! Goddamn!"

Before Nyka could check on her friend, Trigga had her firmly in his grip. "We need to

go...now...Ms. Nyka," he said
weakly. "She'll be okay, but you
won't if we don't go."

Nyka looked at Red, clutching
her arm, but still alive, and
looked back at Trigga. She knew
what she had to do.

"Get out of here, KD," she
whispered to her sudden friend.

Nyka took one last look at Red
before she ran out the door with
Trigga. Whatever happened, her
life was now in his hands.

CHAPTER EIGHTEEN

VEEDA

Veeda couldn't help but to laugh through her busted lips. Turn a nigga's nose up to the right pussy, and he wouldn't even die right.

Fuck Trigga. She'd gotten him good. There wasn't a chance he'd last long with that wound, and by now that Nyka bitch should be with Wild, signing away her property, or dead. At this point, it didn't even matter which to Veeda.

One way or another, Dante's, the land around it, the money connected to it, and soon after all of GCM, would be hers. She tried to toy with Trigga when she could've just killed him.

If he somehow survived, she wouldn't make that mistake any more.

Veeda washed up her face and got herself together. She found her phone in the wreckage of the living room and texted Wild.

She waited, tapping her foot impatiently. She texted again and waited. Then she called. Still nothing. Mutha. Fucker.

Niggas couldn't do anything the way they were supposed to. But it was alright. Her plan, her responsibility. She took a second to compose herself, to get her mind right, her story straight, and she made a call.

"Where the FUCK have you been, Veeda?" Crux's voice boomed from the speaker. "Ain't nobody answering me. Not you, not Trigga, not Wild! Y'all must have me mistaken for some else!"

"I'm so sorry, baby, but things have gotten out of control down here," Veeda said in her most desperate voice. "We're going to have to do something about Trigga."

"The fuck you mean? Explain that shit."

"He's gone completely off the rez. Muthafucker just tried to kill me after I explained to him that he needed to finish his job."

"What?!"

"You heard me, Horatio. He's already tried to kill Wild, he

tried to kill me, and he promised that he wouldn't even let you stand in the way of him and his 'woman of fate'," she said, laying it on thick.

There was a moment of silence. "I don't believe you," Crux said, voice noticeably lower and softer.

"For what reason would I have to lie to you, baby?" Veeda made sure to let her voice quake, as if she were holding back tears. "You've always known how he is about that voodoo shit. You might give commands, but it's his tea leaves and chicken bones that control his actions. Well now that voodoo shit done given him something that's more important

than you and GCM. I don't think
he's coming back. And you and I
both know he can't just leave."

"GCM for life."

"GCM for life."

"Fuck!" she could hear the
pain in Crux's voice, and she
relished it. Trigga and Crux might
be just cousins, but they thought
of themselves as brothers. "My
mama tried to warm me, but I
didn't want to believe it. Okay,
you hold it down for now. Get this
deal back on track any way you
can. I wanted to do this the easy
way, but if I have to get dirty, I
will. Track down anyone and
everyone connected to that Nyka

chick, and pound the information out of them."

"If that's what you want, but I'm telling you, Trigga probably has her gone with the wind," she replied, conveniently leaving out the fact that he was probably dead.

"That's alright. They can't get far. I keep track of all my hitters. If Trigga is with that chick, I'll find them both, no prob."

"Okay," she said, satisfied. "But I think things would go much easier if you came here. We need our heavy hitter here if things are going to get done right."

"Alright, bet. I'm leaving right now, and I'll bring a team with me."

"I'll be waiting." Click. Veeda smiled. Stroke a nigga's ego the right way, and he'd point his gun any way you wanted.

And pretty soon, she'd have one pointed straight at him.

To Be Continued

LOVED THE STORY? Then sign up <u>HERE</u> to receive updates on new releases!

<<<<>>>>

Made in the USA
Columbia, SC
22 February 2019